D1010898

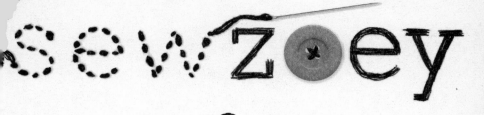

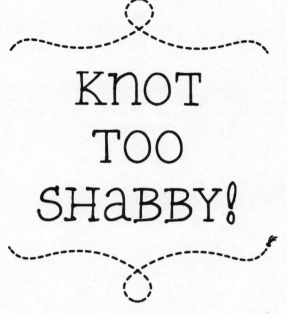

KNOT
TOO
SHABBY!

written by
Chloe Taylor

illustrated by
Nancy Zhang

Simon Spotlight
New York London Toronto Sydney New Delhi

SIMON SPOTLIGHT
An imprint of Simon & Schuster Children's Publishing Division
1230 Avenue of the Americas, New York, New York 10020
Copyright © 2014 by Simon & Schuster, Inc.
All rights reserved, including the right of reproduction in whole or
in part in any form.
SIMON SPOTLIGHT and colophon are registered trademarks of
Simon & Schuster, Inc.
Text by Sarah Darer Littman
Designed by Laura Roode
For information about special discounts for bulk purchases, please contact Simon &
Schuster Special Sales at 1-866-506-1949 or business@simonandschuster.com.
Manufactured in the United States of America 0514 FFG
First Edition 10 9 8 7 6 5 4 3 2 1
ISBN 978-1-4814-1398-5 (pb)
ISBN 978-1-4814-1399-2 (hc)
ISBN 978-1-4814-1400-5 (eBook)
The Library of Congress has catalogued this title.

CHAPTER 1

Fun in the Sun!

I can't believe how fast this school year has flown by! Summer vacation is just around the corner, and so far I'm planning on spending as much time as possible at Camp Lulu and the pool. It seems like only yesterday I got the text message from Priti, just before school started, telling me that our new principal, Ms. Austen, ended the uniform policy and made my dreams come true. I still get excited, just thinking about it. ☺ Yay, Ms. Austen!

But so much has happened since then. I started my Sew Zoey blog, thinking only my family and a few friends would read it, or maybe no one at all. But it really took off, and through my blog I've "met" all of you awesometastic readers and learned so much from you. Sew Zoey has led to things I wouldn't have imagined in my wildest dreams, like being picked for a *Très Chic* website feature and starting online shops for dog (and human) clothes!

I won't pretend it's *all* been fun and games. Sometimes it's been a teensy bit overwhelming. And that, my friends, is the understatement of the century. But I wouldn't trade this year for *anything*. I can't wait to see what new adventures this summer will bring! I just hope it involves plenty of fun in the sun at the beach, which happened to have inspired this sketch.

"This is my favorite day of the school year," Kate Mackey said as she and Zoey Webber waited for

Ms. Brown, their language arts teacher, to pass out their yearbooks. "I love the first time we get to look through the yearbook."

Zoey loved getting her yearbook too, but she wasn't sure she'd go as far as saying it was her *favorite* day of the school year.

"I'm always afraid that there won't be any pictures of me or that there will be a picture of me but an awful one," Zoey said.

"You worry too much, Zo," Kate said. "I bet there will be a picture of you, and you'll look fab in it."

Ms. Brown handed Kate her book and checked off her name against her list.

"And here you go, Zoey," she said, handing over her yearbook. "Planning on launching any exciting new businesses this summer?"

"No," Zoey said. "I need a rest from all ones I started during the school year!"

"Keep at it," encouraged Ms. Brown. "I think it's wonderful you're following your passion."

"I will," Zoey said. "But *after* I spend some time at the pool!"

They didn't have long to look through their

yearbooks before Ms. Brown started class—only as long as it took her to give out the rest of the books to the students.

"Look, Zo! There's a great picture of you, me, Priti, and Libby on the dance floor," Kate said. "And we're all wearing the tiaras you made us."

"You mean from the Sadie Hawkins dance?" Zoey asked.

"Yeah—look!"

It *was* a great picture. They'd all worried so much about asking a boy to the dance, but in the end they'd had the best time going together as a group—four besties being one another's "dates."

It wasn't until lunchtime that Zoey and her friends had the time to really check out the yearbook.

"Oh my gosh, Zoey. Did you see you were voted Best Dressed?" Libby Flynn exclaimed.

"No way! What page? Show me!" Zoey shrieked.

Libby passed her yearbook to Zoey, opened to the awards section. Sure enough, there were several pictures of Zoey wearing her own homemade fashion creations.

"I can't believe it!" Zoey said.

"Why not?" Priti Holbrooke asked. "You always wear cool clothes!"

"I don't know," Zoey said. "I guess because . . . well, because it means that not everyone feels the same way about my outfits as Ivy Wallace does."

"Of course they don't!" Kate said. "Look how many people read your blog."

"And you were asked to be a guest judge on *Fashion Showdown!*" Priti reminded her. "That doesn't happen to just anyone. Especially someone who doesn't have fashion sense."

"Ivy Wallace is just jealous," Libby said. "I bet that's why she always says mean things."

"Still, it's nice to know everyone *else* thinks I'm well-dressed," Zoey said, flipping through the pages of her yearbook. "Hey, look! Priti, you've been voted Most Entertaining!"

"Entertaining? *Moi?* Really?" Priti said, waving her hands in a dramatic gesture.

Zoey passed Priti her yearbook so she could see the picture of herself wearing a glittery headband, with jazz hands and a big smile.

"Why, yes, I guess I *am* the Most Entertaining!" she said. "But where is my Oscar statuette?"

"It's probably still getting engraved." Zoey played along.

Priti giggled.

"Kate, you've been voted Most Likely to Win Olympic Gold!" Libby said, still flipping through the yearbook pages. There were several pictures of Ka* —playing soccer and on the swim team.

Kate blushed as she looked at the pictures. "I don't know why. There are lots of good athletes—"

"C'mon, girl—own it!" Priti said. "You're the bomb!"

"You deserve it," Zoey said. "Mapleton Prep wouldn't have done nearly as well in soccer or swimming without you."

"I guess," Kate said. "But—"

"No buts!" Libby said.

"Own it!" Zoey said.

"Okay, okay, I own it," Kate said.

"Say 'I am the bomb,'" Priti instructed.

"Do I have to?" Kate sighed.

"Yes," Libby said.

Zoey agreed with Priti too. Kate sighed again.

"Oooookay. *I'mthebomb*. Satisfied?" Kate said.

"It's a start, but next time, say it like you really *mean* it," Priti said.

"What about you, Libby?" Kate asked, trying desperately to change the subject from herself. "Did you get an award?"

They all flipped through the awards pages. Sadly, Libby hadn't been voted "best" anything.

"I don't mind," Libby said, "really. Besides, I'm still pretty new here. There's time for me to be best at something."

"Wait, look," Zoey exclaimed. "There's a big picture of you at the fashion show!"

"Ooh, and I'm modeling the dress you made!" Libby said. "Which is still my favorite dress ever, by the way. Well, next to the Libby dress."

"My favorite picture in the whole yearbook is the one of all four of us together," Kate said, turning to the picture of the four girls at the dance, wearing their tiaras.

"Yes!" Priti exclaimed. "I love that one. That was such a fun night."

"That's my favorite, too," Libby said.

"Mine too," Zoey said. "You guys definitely get my vote for Best Besties!"

That night before dinner, Zoey's dad said he had some good news for Zoey.

Zoey was always up for good news.

"I spoke to Erica Hill today," her father said, "and we talked about setting a date for the visit."

Zoey was confused.

"Who is Erica Hill, and what visit?" she asked.

Mr. Webber grinned. "Erica Hill is the assistant to a fashion designer by the name of Daphne Shaw. I think you might have heard of her."

"We're going to visit Daphne's fashion design studio? *Yippeeeee!*" Zoey shrieked. "It's really happening? I'm meeting my idol?"

"Huh? I can't hear you. Um . . . I think you just broke my eardrums," Marcus, Zoey's older brother, complained.

"Sorry, Marcus," Zoey said. "But . . . it's Daphne Shaw!! Can you blame me for being excited? When are we going, Dad? When?"

"The Friday after school gets out," Dad explained. "Erica and I actually talked about the visit a while back, but we agreed it would make more sense to wait till the summer, when you were out of school and the studio wasn't so busy. Daphne wanted to make sure she has time to show you around personally and take you out to lunch."

Zoey hugged her dad and then started dancing around the kitchen in excitement, singing a little victory song. "I'm going to New Yo-orrrk, to meet Daphne Sha-awww!" she sang. "She's taking me to lu-unnnch!"

"I'm going to go cray-zee if Zo-eeey doesn't stop sing-innng," Marcus sang in a groaning parody of his sister. "Dad, please. Make. It. *Sto-oppp!*"

"Actually, I was wondering, Zoey . . ." Her dad hesitated, and Zoey stopped dancing and singing because he sounded serious. "Well, I can drive you to New York and take you to the studio . . . It's just, well, you know what my fashion sense is like. On a scale of one to ten, it's a negative five."

"Negative five is being way too hard on yourself, Dad. I'd have said you were at least a three. I'd even go as high as a four or a five when you aren't wearing sweats," Zoey joked.

"Well, since we're going to the fashion district, to meet a top designer who is your inspiration, the last thing I want to do is embarrass you by showing up in some fuddy-duddy outfit. So what do you say we hit the mall tonight, and you can help me pick out a more *fashion-forward* outfit?"

"Yes! I'd be happy to be your fashion adviser," Zoey said, giving her father another hug. It was really kind of cute when he admitted he was prone to making fashion faux pas. She couldn't wait to take him shopping!

Later that night, Marcus and his band were practicing in the basement. Mr. Webber ordered them pizza for dinner so that he and Zoey could get an early start at the mall. It began raining as they headed to the car.

"You can have your pick of the food court," Dad said as they pulled out of the garage.

"After we find you an outfit," Zoey corrected. "Fashion comes first!"

"I should have known." Dad sighed. "Duds before grub."

Rain pelted down on the roof of the car so hard that Zoey almost had to shout to be heard.

"It better not be like this when school gets out," Zoey complained. "My friends and I have important poolside plans, and the pool and the pouring rain don't mix."

"Don't worry, Zo," her dad said. "It's probably just a passing downpour."

Sure enough, by the time they got to the mall, the rain had lightened to a drizzle and the setting sun was trying to peek its way through the clouds on the horizon.

"Look, Dad, a rainbow!" Zoey exclaimed.

"Even better, a double rainbow," her dad said. "That's extra good luck."

"If I have much more good luck, I might explode from excitement," Zoey said.

"Well, let's go get me properly attired," Dad said. "I don't want to break your streak and embarrass you on the big day."

Zoey wasn't sure if shopping for her dad was

going to be as much fun as shopping for herself and her friends, but giving him a makeover turned out to be really fun. Like when he went for his favorite style of pants and shirts and she took them out of his hands and put them right back.

"Nuh-uh, Dad. This is a *makeover*, not a *make the same fashion choices over and over*," she said. "Don't forget, we're going to the heart of the fashion capital. You need to up your game."

Instead, she made him try on some straight-leg black jeans, a button-down shirt with a bold stripe, and a sleek blazer. When he came out of the dressing room, she clapped.

"Wow, Dad! Welcome to the twenty-first century!" Zoey said, smiling. "You look amazing."

Mr. Webber checked himself out in the mirror.

"I have to admit, I would never in a million years have picked this stuff to try on, but now that I have, I like the way it looks."

"That's why you need me," Zoey told him. "To guide you to better fashion choices."

Her father smiled at her in the mirror.

"You're right, honey. I do need you. From now

on, consider yourself my official fashion guru."

"We're not done yet, Dad. You need a new belt and shoes, too."

By the time they walked out of the store, Mr. Webber had a complete Zoey-approved outfit from top to toe. Zoey even picked out some new dress socks with a subtle pattern.

"I feel like a new man," Mr. Webber declared. "But at this point, I'm a very hungry new man. Where do you want to go for dinner?"

Zoey picked a popular burger place she knew her dad liked too.

After the waitress had taken their order, her dad suddenly had on what Zoey thought of as his "serious discussion face."

"Zo, I need to ask you something," he said.

Zoey fiddled with the straw in her water glass, hoping it wasn't going to be something awkward.

"What's that, Dad?"

"I want to make sure you're okay with me taking you to New York," Dad said. "Aunt Lulu would have loved to go, you know, and maybe visit some interior design studios while you guys were up there. I know she also would have loved to have done the whole shopping thing with you. The problem is, she's got a big deadline, and she just can't afford to take the time off right now."

"It's okay, Dad," Zoey said. "I'm happy you're taking me."

Her father looked surprised, but Zoey could tell he was also relieved.

"You are?"

"Yeah. I mean, I know fashion isn't your thing, exactly," Zoey started.

"That's putting it mildly." Dad laughed.

"But, really—I'm glad you can be part of my big day visiting Daphne," Zoey said. "I always wonder what it would be like to share with Mom all the great stuff that's happened with Sew Zoey. And if you come, I know you'll tell me what you think she'd have said and what she'd have done—it's like having both of you rolled into one. Plus, it'll be fun to have some daddy-daughter time."

For a moment, Zoey thought her dad was going to get all mushy, as he sometimes did when Zoey talked about her mom, who passed away when Zoey was a toddler. But he just smiled, took her hand, and squeezed it tight.

"Well, I'm glad you're okay with it, because I'm looking forward to being a part of your big day, too," he said. "And by the way, I know Mom would have been so proud of you and everything you've accomplished with Sew Zoey. Just like I am."

CHAPTER 2

A Surprise Prize at the End of the Rainbow

Yesterday, when I left for the mall with Dad, it was pouring, but by the time we got there it was starting to clear, and I saw a rainbow. Better yet, it wasn't just any rainbow—it was a *double rainbow*! Dad told me that while rainbows are lucky, double rainbows are doubly lucky! I think he must be right because I found out that one of my dreams is coming true this summer . . . but I can't tell my Sew Zoey readers until I've told my BFFs. What's the prize at the end of my rainbow? It's not a leprechaun or a pot of gold—it's way better than that! I'm sorry to be so secretive, but I promise to share more details as soon as I can!

It looks like this summer is already shaping up to be pretty amazing—and school hasn't even ended yet. I wonder what else is on the horizon!

Zoey was bursting to tell her friends about the visit to Daphne's studio, but she wanted to wait until they were all together at lunch. When she sat down, Kate was already talking about which sports camps she was attending.

"Soccer camp in Pennsylvania, and then I'm home for, like, one day to do laundry, and then I head straight out the door again to go to the Adirondacks for swimming and riding and general sports camp."

"So you're gone for most of the summer?" Priti asked.

"Pretty much," Kate admitted. "I'll miss you guys a lot, but I have to admit, I love camp. It's so much fun. And I'll be back in August."

"Really? You love camp?" Priti sighed. "My parents are nagging me to go to this theater sleepaway camp this summer. And I mean *nonstop* nagging. They're like, 'Priti, it will be such a great experience for you!' and 'Priti, you'll make new friends!' But I don't know if I want to go."

"Maybe you could try a short session to test it out," Kate suggested.

"Maybe," Priti said, but she sounded dubious. "Are you going anywhere, Libby?"

"I'm going to ballet camp," Libby said. "But it's not a sleepaway camp. Just a day camp."

"I wouldn't mind day camp as much," Priti said. "It feels like my parents are desperate to get rid of me!"

"I'm sure that's not true, Priti," Zoey assured her.

"I know," Priti said. "But when they nag me to go away for the whole summer every single day, it sure feels like they are! It makes it hard to get excited about it."

"Well, I'm superexcited for the weekend after next," Libby jumped in, "because before camp starts, I'm going up to New York for a special weekend with my aunt Lexie! You know, the one who's a buyer for H. Cashin's, the department store?"

"Wait, you are?" Zoey exclaimed. "I'm going to New York that weekend too!"

"Really? That's awesome," Libby said. "What are you going up there for?"

"Well . . . that's what I've been waiting to tell you guys," Zoey said.

"Wait! Is this the surprise you were talking about on your blog?" Priti asked. "I love that rainbow dress, by the way!"

"Yes!" Zoey said, then added, "And thanks! So . . . I'm going to New York to meet DAPHNE SHAW!!"

"No way!" Libby squealed.

"Yes!! *Way!* I'm going to spend the whole day at her design studio! She's even going to take me out for lunch," Zoey said. "It's like a dream come true."

"I'm so happy for you, Zo," Kate said.

"You weren't kidding on your blog, then. That really *is* better than a pot of gold at the end of the rainbow," Priti said. "How did it happen?"

"Do you remember when I was getting all those nasty comments on Sew Zoey?" Zoey asked.

"Yes." Kate nodded. "And it turned out to be Ivy, Shannon, and Bree using lots of different fake screen names."

Ivy Wallace, Shannon Chang, and Bree Sharpe were some not-so-nice girls who went to Mapleton Prep.

"That's right. Well, remember how Daphne wrote a comment on my blog about how creative people have to get used to criticism because art is subjective and reminded me about *sticks and stones*?"

"How could we forget?" Priti said. "That was supermega-exciting!"

"Well, she invited me then, and I wanted to go right away, but I couldn't because of school."

"How could you stand waiting?" Priti demanded.

"Well, to tell you the truth, I got so busy with Doggie Duds and everything else that I kind of forgot about it for a while," Zoey confessed. "But Dad talked to her assistant about setting a date for when school ended, and I'm going next Friday!"

"Really? I'm going from Thursday night through Sunday," Libby said. "Aunt Lexie's taken Friday off from work for a special treat she's got planned." She paused, thinking for a moment. "What if . . . It would be fun if we went to New York together and you spent the weekend with me and Aunt Lexie, wouldn't it? I'd have to check that it's okay with her, but what do you think? Maybe we can all go!"

Zoey had met Libby's aunt when they went to an accessories show and had really liked her. Spending a weekend with her and Libby in New York sounded fabulous.

"That sounds like fun," Kate said. "Wish I could join you, but I'll have already left for camp."

"I won't have," Priti said. "Even if my parents force me to go, camp's not for another few weeks."

"Cool! I'll call Aunt Lexie tonight and ask if it's okay to bring friends," Libby said. "It would be so much fun for all three of us to go together. My mom can drive us."

"And I'll check with Dad," Zoey said. "I hope he says yes!"

It wasn't until she got home and was waiting impatiently for her father to return from work so she could ask him that it suddenly struck Zoey that maybe Dad would be upset if she wanted to go to New York with Libby instead of with him. After all, he'd gone to all the trouble of asking her to take him shopping for a special "cool Dad" outfit, just so he wouldn't embarrass her at Daphne's studio. The last thing she wanted to do was hurt his feelings.

The truth was, Zoey had been looking forward to their daddy-daughter day in the city. But the prospect of a weekend-long slumber party with her friends and Libby's aunt Lexie sounded like so much fun! She didn't want Dad to be upset, but she didn't want to miss out on a good time, either. What should she do?

After her father came home, Zoey waited until they'd all sat down to dinner to broach the question, when he was more relaxed.

"Guess what, Dad? It turns out Libby is going to visit her aunt Lexie the exact same weekend as I'm supposed to go tour Daphne Shaw's studio. She has to check with her aunt first, but she thought it would be fun for us to have a slumber party at her aunt's apartment for the weekend." Zoey wasn't sure, but she thought she caught a look of disappointment flash across her father's face. "So . . . what do you think?"

Mr. Webber put down his fork slowly and carefully. When he looked up at Zoey, he smiled.

"That's a great idea, honey," he said. "I'm sure you girls will have a blast . . . as long as it's okay with Libby's aunt."

Zoey breathed a sigh of relief. She didn't want her father to be mad or upset about not going—but she wanted to have fun with Libby, too!

"Zo's having a girl's weekend in the city?" Marcus asked. "I need a boy's weekend. I still haven't been to Rudy's Music Stop."

"We'll have a boys weekend sometime soon," Dad promised. "I'll take you to Rudy's Music Stop, and you can eat all the New York pizza you want."

"Sounds like a slice of heaven," Marcus said.

"Dad, I just thought of something," Zoey said. "What if Lexie can't take me to Daphne's studio? Libby said she's taken Friday off from work for a special treat for Libby. Maybe she has big plans."

"Let's just take this one step at a time," Dad said. "We don't even know if Libby's aunt has agreed to this yet. I'll call Mrs. Flynn tonight and ask for Lexie's phone number, so we can work out the logistics tomorrow."

"Okay," Zoey said.

She really hoped things worked out. In the meantime, she kept thinking of how much fun it was going to be hanging out in the city with Libby and Priti and Libby's aunt Lexie. She couldn't wait!

Later that evening, Zoey and her father were watching TV when the phone rang. Mr. Webber picked up, and after saying hello and listening for a minute, he went into the kitchen, obviously not wanting Zoey to hear, which of course made her more curious. She decided to go get herself a glass of milk, and when she went into the kitchen, he was still on the phone. "No, Zoey doesn't—"

He spotted her and stopped speaking. The expression on his face made Zoey anxious. . . .

Who was he talking to? Was there a hitch in the

weekend plans? Or was her dad more upset about her bailing on their daddy-daughter day than he was letting on?

She took her glass of milk out to the living room. When her dad came back, he settled onto the sofa and asked her what he'd missed on the TV show. She told him and then asked, "Is everything okay?"

"Sure, honey. Why wouldn't it be?" her dad asked.

Zoey shrugged.

She still felt uneasy.

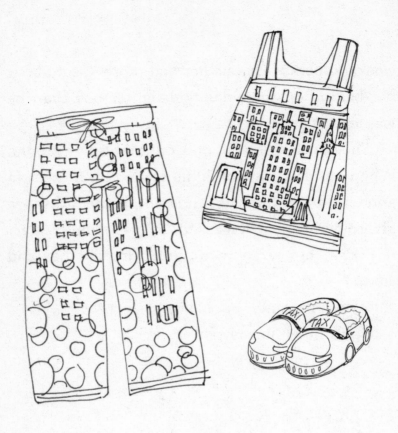

-------- CHAPTER 3 --------

Slumber Party in the Big Apple

I can tell you my big secret now! I'm going to visit the design studio of none other than my fashion idol—*drumroll, please*—DAPHNE SHAW!! Can you believe it?! I have to keep pinching myself so *I* do.

To make things even more exciting, I might be

having a sleepover party in the big city with my friends that same weekend. I've designed these NYC-inspired pajamas for myself and am making them tonight, but the funky slippers are just an idea for now. I've learned a lot since I started sewing, but I have no idea how to make slippers!

I hope it all works out, because while our slumber parties in Mapleton are fun, a slumber party in the Big Apple would be a really great way to start the summer, don't you think? Here's to summer—or *slumber*—in the city!

"Okay, you guys, I've got good news and bad news," Libby announced at lunch the next day. "Which do you want first?"

"I could use some good news with everything going on with my parents," Priti said. "Let's have that first."

"Well, the good news is that Aunt Lexie was okay about me inviting a friend," Libby said. "But that's also the bad news. She's got a really small apartment, and she said she can really only handle two tween girls there at a time." Libby looked from Zoey to Priti and then back again. "I feel really awful about this. What do we do?"

Zoey and Priti exchanged glances. Zoey really wanted to go with Libby, but the last thing she wanted to do was upset Priti, especially after Priti said she needed some good news. Things had been difficult between Priti's parents for a while now. *Maybe I should just let Priti go with Libby, and I'll go with Dad as we'd originally planned,* Zoey thought.

She was just about to open her mouth to suggest that when Priti spoke up.

"Zoey should go," she said. "After all, she's got an actual reason to be in New York next weekend. I just wanted to tag along because it sounded like fun."

"Are . . . you sure?" Zoey asked. "Because my dad can still take me if you really want to go."

"I'm sure," Priti said. "Come on, Zo. You're going to see *Daphne Shaw*! You deserve to have a totally awesome weekend."

Zoey reached over and hugged her friend.

"You're the best BFF ever, Priti," she said. "I was just about to ask you if you wanted to go instead."

"Which makes you a great BFF too," Priti said. "But I do have a price for my BFF-iness."

"Which is . . . ?" Libby asked.

"Cupcakes!" Priti said, smiling. "I want a cupcake from Sugar Sweet Sunshine in the Lower East Side. It's the most amazing cupcake bakery in the entire universe. OMG, they are so good. I'll take a Sassy Red Velvet cupcake. No, wait, an Ooey Gooey cupcake. No, a—"

"We'll bring you an assortment," Libby said. "Then you can try them all."

"Now I'm starting to wish I was going to be home instead of at camp," Kate said. "I mean . . . I just had lunch, but those cupcakes are making me hungry again!"

"We'll have another cupcake party when you get back," Zoey said. "A 'Welcome Home, Kate' cupcake party."

"Sounds like a plan," Kate said. "A yummy plan!"

Zoey was relieved that everything seemed to be working out for the big weekend without anyone getting really upset. Priti seemed content with the promise of her favorite cupcakes from Sugar Sweet Sunshine, and Dad . . . Well, he said he was okay with not going, but Zoey wasn't 100 percent sure she believed him after seeing him looking so serious on the phone the night before.

Still, Zoey was so excited for her weekend slumber party with Libby that it was hard to concentrate for the rest of the afternoon in school. She kept imagining all the fun things they were going to do in New York. When Zoey's imagination was on the loose, she couldn't help doodling too.

Luckily, with there being less than a week of school left, there wasn't that much going on in class, so she only got called out once for daydreaming.

Mr. Webber was home early that evening and speaking on the phone when Zoey got home from school.

"Great! We'll look forward to seeing you next Friday, late afternoon. And thanks again for agreeing to host Zoey!" he said before hanging up the phone.

He seemed in a much better mood than he'd been in the night before.

"Hi, Dad," Zoey said. "Who was that?"

"That was Libby's aunt Lexie," Dad said. "There's been a slight change of plans."

Zoey's face must have given away her worry that the sleepover was off because her father said, "Don't worry, Zo! You still get to spend the weekend with Libby."

"Oh, good," Zoey said.

"Now, I have to trust you to keep this part a secret, because it's a surprise for Libby. Can you do that?" her dad asked.

"Ookay," Zoey agreed, wondering what was so hush-hush.

"Aunt Lexie can't take you to Daphne's studio on Friday because she planned a surprise spa day for her and Libby in the morning—and visits to some art galleries in the afternoon. Promise you won't tell Libby?"

"I won't," Zoey promised.

"So, instead of you going on Thursday with Libby and her mother, I'll drive you on Friday as we'd originally planned, drop you at Daphne's studio, stay for a bit—and then I'll meet an old college friend for lunch," Dad explained. "When you're done at Daphne's, I'll take you to Lexie's apartment. Then Libby's mom will drive you home on Sunday. How does that sound?"

"It sounds perfect!" Zoey exclaimed. "It's the best of both worlds."

She hugged her father. "I'm glad you're going to be taking me to Daphne's. I would have missed having our daddy-daughter time—and besides, you look so snazzy in your new outfit!"

Mr. Webber brushed a stray lock of hair back from Zoey's face.

"I'm glad we're going to have our Dad and Zoey time too. The last thing I want is for you to miss out on fun times with your friends, but . . . I'm happy it all worked out so I get to be a part of your big day too."

"Now I have to figure out what to *wear*." Zoey sighed. "I mean, this is *Daphne Shaw* we're talking about here."

"I'm the last person who can help you with that problem," her father said, grinning. "You better dial 1-800-AUNT-LULU for *that* kind of advice."

Before Zoey knew it, the last day of school arrived. Nobody was even pretending to do any work. Teachers either let the students watch movies or sign yearbooks. In language arts, Zoey asked Lorenzo Romy, the boy she'd had a crush earlier in the year, to sign hers.

"Sure," he said, taking it from her, scribbling his name and "Have an awesome summer!" and then handing it back.

Even though she and Lorenzo were just friends, Zoey thought he would have written something a little more thoughtful than that. She stood for a moment, waiting for him to ask her to sign his, but he didn't. Shrugging, she turned and walked back to her desk.

"Hey, Zoey, can I get the autograph of Mapleton Prep's most celebrated student for my yearbook?"

Gabe Monaco, the boy who'd sat in front of her all year, was holding out his yearbook and a pen.

"Celebrated?" Ivy retorted, leaning over her desk to interrupt. "Are you sure you don't mean 'dorky'?"

Gabe kept his eyes on Zoey. "No, I'm pretty sure

I meant 'celebrated,' as in well-known, respected, and admired," he said.

"Well, in that case, you can definitely have my autograph," Zoey said. "As long as you autograph my yearbook too."

Ivy muttered something about "nerd love," but Zoey ignored her as she gave Gabe her yearbook. His cheeks were tinged pink. She reminded herself that Ivy might think Zoey was dorky, but the rest of the student body had voted her Best Dressed. Maybe it was true what Libby said about Ivy just being jealous.

Now, what should she write in Gabe's yearbook? She wanted to write more than "Have an awesome summer!" Gabe made her laugh and always stuck up for her when Ivy was being a pain. He was also a lot more fun to dance with than Lorenzo, as she had discovered at a school dance.

In the end, she sketched a picture of him sitting at his desk with her behind him, sending a paper airplane that was trailing a banner that read: HOPE WE'RE IN CLASS TOGETHER AGAIN NEXT YEAR! YOUR "CELEBRATED" FRIEND, ZOEY.

Gabe took even longer than she did, even though he was writing slowly. He looked like he was thinking about each word before he wrote it.

"Are you writing a book?" Zoey teased.

"No," he said. "Just . . . a little something."

The bell rang as soon as Gabe gave back her yearbook, so it wasn't until she was sitting next to Libby in art class that she was able to see what he'd written:

To Zoey—who always makes life more interesting and colorful. I've really enjoyed being in class with you this year. Hope you have a great summer. I'll miss you.

Looking forward to seeing you next year,

Gabe

"*Interesting and colorful,*" Zoey repeated to herself. "*I'll miss you?*" Now she was the one with the pink-tinged cheeks.

"Libby," Zoey said, showing her Gabe's inscription. "What does he mean by 'colorful'? That's a compliment, right?"

"Definitely, especially coming from Gabe!" Libby said. "I think he might have a crush on you."

Zoey really liked Gabe. But in a way she was glad summer vacation was about to start. She wasn't sure if she was ready for any more crush dramas right now. After an action-packed year, she just wanted to relax, enjoy the summer, and have fun with her friends.

During math, Zoey was called down to Ms. Austen's office. Usually, she wondered if she'd done something wrong if she got called to the principal's office, but she was pretty sure her slate was clean. Besides, it was the last day of school. Ms. Austen was hardly likely to be giving her a detention!

"This came for you," Ms. Austen said when Zoey arrived, handing her a small padded envelope. "I think it's from your friend Fashionsista. It's lucky it came today, isn't it? Just in the nick of time."

"I know!" Zoey said, opening the envelope. Inside was an adorable pincushion shaped like a hedgehog, attached to a cuff bracelet so it could be worn on her wrist. The pins looked like the hedgehog's little spikes. Zoey slipped it on her wrist and admired it.

"Ooh, it's so cute, isn't it?" she said, showing it off to Ms. Austen.

"It is adorable. Practical, too," Ms. Austen said. "It's much easier to pin a hem when you're wearing the pincushion on your wrist."

Zoey took the note out of the envelope and read it aloud:

Dear Zoey,

I was in England recently, and when I saw this, I thought you'd get a kick out of it. Congratulations on a beyond-successful year of school and best wishes for an exciting summer!

Your friend,
Fashionsista

"That's so nice of her!" Zoey exclaimed.

"It really is," Ms. Austen said. "You're very lucky to have a friend like her. She seems to have taken a special interest in you."

"It's amazing. I wish I knew who she was, you know, so I could thank her in person," Zoey said, "instead of just writing to her on my blog. Plus, I'm dying of curiosity!"

"Aren't we all?" Ms. Austen chuckled.

At the end of the day, when the final bell rang, everyone cheered. Zoey emptied the things from her locker into her book bag, and, overloaded, went out front to find Priti. Zoey's dad had left work a little early and was picking up Zoey and Priti from school as a treat. When Zoey found Priti, Mr. Webber had already arrived and was talking to Ms. Austen by the entrance.

Zoey stopped for a minute and watched them before they caught sight of her. Dad was wearing his new jeans and looked younger than he usually did. But there was something odd about the way he and Ms. Austen were chatting. She couldn't quite put her finger on it.

"Zo . . . is it my imagination or are your dad and Ms. Austen really . . . *smiley* with each other all of a sudden?" Priti asked.

Zoey stared at Priti, wide-eyed, as she contemplated what that might mean and looked back at her dad and Ms. Austen.

Is that it?

"Um . . . yeah, they are. But . . . maybe it's just because it's the last day of school and they're in a good mood or something."

"Yeah. Maybe," Priti said. But she didn't sound completely convinced.

When the girls walked up, Zoey's dad and Ms. Austen smiled at the two of them. Zoey's dad grabbed the girls' heavy backpacks while Ms. Austen wished them both a good summer.

"Enjoy meeting Daphne Shaw," Ms. Austen said to Zoey. "I can't wait to read all about it on Sew Zoey."

CHAPTER 4

Knotty and Very Nice

School is officially over! And on the last day, I received the cutest hedgehog-shaped pincushion from Fashionsista. Thank you sooo much! I love it. In fact, I'm wearing it on my wrist right now as I type, even though I'm not sewing anything! I googled hedgehogs, and they are the most adorable little creatures—and useful, too, because they eat garden pests.

I'm having a hard time eating anything right now—my stomach is tied up in knots about the upcoming visit to Daphne Shaw's studio. I keep running through various scenarios in my head, trying to think of what I'll say so that I won't sound like a total fashion newbie. The problem is, I don't have any idea what to expect. But if Ms. Shaw is by any chance taking time out of her busy schedule to read this blog post, please don't take this the wrong way—I'm nervous, yes, but I'm also SUPER DUPER EXCITED, and the excited part is definitely outweighing the nervous part!

"I can't believe we're on our way!" Zoey exclaimed as the car whizzed under a New York directional sign on the highway. "I'm going to meet DAPHNE SHAW!!"

"It's pretty exciting, isn't it?" her dad said, smiling. "Am I fashionable enough in my new duds to accompany you?"

"You'll pass," Zoey said. "In fact, you might just be a trendsetter!"

"Well, you look great too, honey," her father said. "I'm so proud of my little girl."

"I'm not so little anymore," Zoey said.

"I know," Dad said. "That's a problem we dads have. Even when you're a grown woman, it'll be hard for me to stop thinking of you as my little girl."

"Promise me you won't say any little girl stuff or do anything else embarrassing in front of Daphne Shaw?"

"Scout's honor," her dad said. "I'll do my best to be the least-embarrassing father alive."

"That's a relief," Zoey said. "Because Daphne Shaw is like the coolest person in the whole fashion industry, and I'm already worried about making a fool of myself."

"You'll do fine, Zo," Dad said. "Just be yourself. Daphne was a young girl just starting out once upon a time too."

It was hard for Zoey to imagine Daphne Shaw as a girl her age. Daphne seemed so confident and sophisticated in her *Très Chic* interviews—not at all like how Zoey felt.

"It's too bad Priti couldn't come to New York

with us," she said. "I think she was really disappointed, even though she said she wasn't."

"I'm sure she was disappointed," Dad said. "But I think she's going to sleepaway camp soon. That should be a fun for her."

"Wait . . . how do *you* know that?" Zoey asked, her brow furrowing with confusion. "Priti told us her parents were nagging her about it, but she wasn't sure she wanted to go."

Her father's face grew serious. It took on the same tense, troubled look he had the week before when she thought he was upset about her going to New York with Libby instead of with him.

"Look, Zo—I don't want to lie to you, but I'm telling you this in confidence. Mr. Holbrooke called me the other night to ask a favor," he said, his hands gripping the steering wheel. "Priti's parents have been trying to encourage her to go to sleepaway camp for two reasons: because they genuinely do think she'll have a good time, but also because they need some time alone to work on their marriage. They're thinking that maybe taking a vacation without the kids—something they haven't done in years—might be a good way to do that."

"But Priti doesn't seem like she wants to go," Zoey said. "She was upset because she felt like her parents were trying to get rid of her."

"Oh, poor Priti—it's not that at all," Dad said. "The Holbrookes just need a little time alone to sort things out. Tara and Sashi already found programs they want to go to, but Priti doesn't want to go away, and I think her parents are worried about telling her the truth. That's why Mr. Holbrooke called me. He thinks Priti would be happier about the idea if she could go with a friend . . . and he asked me if you'd be willing to go. I told him I'd have to talk to you—I'm not going to force you, but I think it could be a really fun experience for the two of you."

Zoey wasn't so sure.

"But Priti said it was a theater camp. Drama is more Priti's thing than mine."

"Actually it's not just a theater camp. It's a fine arts camp, and they also have the usual camp activities, like canoeing and campfires," her dad explained. "They're holding two spaces for you and Priti. If you decide to go, then you'd leave in two weeks and do a six-week session. What do you think?"

"Can I think about it?" Zoey asked.

"Sure, honey—I know I just sprang this on you. I told Mr. Holbrooke I'd let him know by Monday morning, so you've got the whole weekend to think about it."

It turned out Zoey didn't need that long to think—because almost immediately, she began to imagine how much fun it could be to go to sleepaway arts camp with Priti. All of those artsy and campy activities *while* having a summer-long sleepover *and* helping Priti's parents work on their marriage? It was a total win-win. Maybe even a win-win-win.

"I'll do it," she told her dad.

"That was quick," he said. "Are you sure?"

"It's okay. It'll be fun. And even if it isn't, if it helps Priti's parents stay together, it'll be worth it."

Zoey's father reached over and gave her hand a squeeze.

"Thanks for being so grown-up about this, Zo. I know you're going to have a great time," her dad said. "I hope it helps the Holbrookes, too. We'll just have to wait and see."

"Priti's really worried about her parents getting divorced. She doesn't always show it, but she is."

"I know, honey. And her parents will really appreciate you being such a good friend to her by giving them time this summer to work on things," Dad said. "I'll call the Holbrookes tonight and tell them you've agreed to go, and also that I've told you the reason why, so they should be honest with Priti and tell her what's going on."

With summer plans to talk about, the rest of the ride passed quickly. It seemed like no time before they were approaching Manhattan, with the New York City skyline laid out before them.

"It looks just like a postcard, doesn't it?" Zoey sighed. "I can hardly believe it's real."

"I know what you mean," her dad said. "Unfortunately, this traffic is all too real. If it doesn't start moving, we're going to be late."

"No! We can't be late!" Zoey panicked. "Not for Daphne Shaw! What will she think?"

"She'll think we got stuck in traffic, which happens all the time," her dad said.

Fortunately, the traffic started moving, and

they made it to a parking garage near Daphne's studio with a little time to spare. As they walked the few blocks to the building, Zoey's head swiveled from one direction to the other as she tried to take in all the cool clothes and funky hairstyles she saw on the street.

Daphne Shaw Atelier was housed in a converted warehouse. The reception area was very modern, light, and airy, thanks to the huge windows and high ceilings. Abstract art and larger-than-life photographs from Daphne's runway shows were hung on exposed brick walls and lit in a way that highlighted them perfectly. Almost everything else was white, even the furniture.

"Aunt Lulu would love this place," Zoey whispered to her dad.

"She sure would," Dad said. Then he nodded in the direction of a young male employee wearing a fedora. "Hey, do you think I'd look good in that?"

"Wow, Dad," Zoey said. "We might just make you a fashion icon yet!"

"Let's not get ahead of ourselves," Dad said. "Baby steps."

"Wow, speaking of baby steps, look at that woman's high heels. I wonder how she walks in them," Zoey confessed, looking in the direction of a woman pushing a garment rack. "I mean, I hope wearing sky-high heels isn't a requirement to work in fashion. I like my comfy Converse!"

"I say wear whatever you want," her dad said. "And high heels can wait."

Seeing all the fashionably dressed employees, Zoey started worrying about her outfit. She was wearing an apple-print sundress she had made in honor of her trip to the Big Apple, a taxi-shaped purse, and ankle-tie flats. She'd felt good about it when she looked in the mirror in her bedroom at home, but here in Daphne Shaw's chic office . . . she wasn't so sure she had made the right choice. She didn't feel grown up at all.

"Hi, you must be Zoey!"

Zoey had been so busy checking out the lobby that she hadn't noticed the petite, dark-haired girl in top-to-toe black who'd come out to greet her.

"Yes . . . that's me," Zoey said. "And this is my dad."

"Hi, Dad," the girl said. "I'm Jessie, one of Daphne's assistants. She's waiting to meet you in her office."

Zoey's heart felt like it skipped a beat. After dreaming about this moment for so long, she was finally going to meet the amazing and inspirational Daphne Shaw, her fashion idol!

They followed Jessie down a long hallway lined with framed photographs and sketches from past collections.

Daphne Shaw's office was at the end of the corridor; a large room with skylights and big windows and crisp, clean, modern design. And right in the middle of it, standing behind her desk, holding up fabric swatches to the light, was Daphne Shaw herself. She was tall and elegant, wearing metallic stilettos, a navy pencil skirt, and a fitted white blazer topped off by a chunky necklace made of geometric persimmon-colored beads.

"Zoey!" Daphne said, coming from behind the desk to give Zoey a brief, scented hug. "What an adorable dress! I'm so happy we finally get to meet in real life. . . . I feel as if I already know you from reading your delightful blog."

Please, mouth, open and speak! Zoey thought. For a moment, she was so awestruck to be in the presence of her greatest fashion inspiration that she wasn't sure if her brain remembered how.

"I am, t-too!" she finally stuttered.

She had a minute to pull herself together while Daphne greeted her father, complimenting him on his fashion sense.

After glancing around the room again, Zoey finally had the courage to speak. "I really love your office, Ms. Shaw."

"Thanks, Zoey, I designed it myself. And, please, call me Daphne."

"Okay, um . . . Daphne," Zoey replied. "Well, would it be okay to take a picture for my aunt? She's an interior designer, and she'd think it was so cool. Also, I don't want to forget one single thing about today."

"Of course," Daphne said. "And feel free to post it on your blog, too."

"Why don't you let me take it so you and Daphne can be in the picture together," Dad suggested.

"Yes—great idea," Daphne agreed.

Zoey gave her father her phone and went to stand next to Daphne in front of her desk.

"Say '*fromage*,'" Dad said.

Daphne laughed and obliged. Zoey was too busy pretending to smile and not cringe as her father took the picture. Why couldn't Dad just say "cheese" like normal fathers?

When her father handed her back the phone, Zoey showed it to Daphne.

"Wonderful! You're very photogenic, Zoey," Daphne said.

Zoey didn't think she looked *that* great in pictures, but she was excited to have a souvenir of her visit to Daphne's office to post on her blog.

"Are you going to join us on the tour of the studio?" Daphne asked Zoey's dad. "You're welcome to stay."

"Actually, I've arranged to meet an old college buddy for lunch," Dad said. "So I'll leave you two to talk fashion."

He gave Zoey a hug.

"Have a great time, honey. See you later."

"Have fun too, Dad," Zoey said.

She had to confess—she was a little relieved her dad wasn't staying. Even the best dads in the world could be embarrassing at times, and she'd already been struck speechless in front of Daphne Shaw. She didn't need any further embarrassment.

"Well, we better get started," Daphne said after Dad left with Jessie. "We've got a busy day ahead of us."

Zoey saw Daphne slipping something shiny into her desk drawer as she said it but couldn't see what it was. She forgot about it almost immediately as she followed Daphne out of her office, down the hallway, and into the showroom, where items from her latest collection were on display. The conference room featured a long, brushed-metal table and comfortable office chairs. The walls were lined with inspiration boards and fabric swatches, sketches, and color palettes. There was a small lunchroom with artistic drawings of vegetables on the walls.

"Did you do those, too?" Zoey asked.

"No, one of my assistants did," Daphne said.

"I liked her drawings so much, I bought them and framed them."

Zoey thought Daphne sounded like a nice boss. She hoped she would be like her someday.

But Zoey's favorite part of the whole studio was the workroom. It was the biggest room of all—light and airy with big tables upon which the sample makers were cutting fabric, and industrial sewing machines where seamstresses were working on pieces. In another part of the workroom, embroiderers put the final touches on sleek, elegant pieces from the fall collection. In yet another corner, a draper worked with fabric on a dress form.

"There's never a dull moment around here. As soon as we finish one collection, it's on to the next one," Daphne explained.

An adorable little Yorkie came trotting over from behind one of the tables and went straight to Daphne, who picked her up. Zoey couldn't believe her eyes because the dog was wearing one of her Doggie Duds creations!

"Zoey, I'd like you to meet my little darling, Coco. She's named after Coco Chanel."

"She's wearing the Buttons!" Zoey exclaimed.

Zoey had designed two styles of dog outfits: one named for Aunt Lulu's late dog, Draper, the inspiration for Doggie Duds, and the other, more feminine version named after Buttons, Aunt Lulu's current dog.

"Yes! I loved your designs so much, I had to order two different versions of the Buttons for Coco," Daphne said. "She loves them, don't you, precious?"

Zoey remembered Daphne had ordered one of her outfits but didn't remember her buying two. How cool! And she couldn't believe Daphne liked them enough to let her dog wear them to the office. She asked Daphne if it was okay to take a picture of her holding Coco, and Daphne agreed. She posed with Coco right there in the middle of her workroom!

Daphne put down Coco and glanced at her watch.

"Have you worked up an appetite yet?" she asked. "I've got lunch reservations for us at a darling little restaurant around the corner."

Zoey realized that she was hungry—starving,

in fact. It had been a long time since she and her dad ate breakfast, but she'd been so excited about everything Daphne was showing her that she hadn't really paid attention to her tummy rumbling.

"Yes, I am," she said.

"Great, let's go eat!" Daphne said.

Zoey was worried that the restaurant would be really fancy and she'd feel out of place, but it turned out to be a homey little Italian spot, with red-and-white checkered tablecloths, filled with the delicious aromas of warm bread, olive oil, and garlic. The owner knew Daphne and kissed her on both cheeks, European style, when she walked in the door.

"This is my very talented young friend Zoey Webber," Daphne introduced, and Zoey thought she might faint with pride. It wasn't every day that you got to hear your fashion idol call you very talented!

"Delighted to meet you, Signorina Webber," the owner said. "I'll take you both to the usual table."

Daphne's usual table was in a small private alcove overlooking the garden in the back of the restaurant, which contained artfully placed planters filled with green shrubs and colorful blooms. It almost made Zoey forget she was in the middle of New York City.

"You know, Zoey, I see a lot of myself in you," Daphne said after they'd ordered. "I started sewing when I was about your age."

"When you were in middle school, did you ever think that you'd be a famous fashion designer like you are now?" Zoey asked.

"Oh, I fantasized about it. But when I was sketching and sewing outfits in my room back in middle school, I would never have believed that I'd have my own studio and fashion line," Daphne said. "Sometimes, I still have to pinch myself because I can't believe I get to live my dream and be successful at it. It just seems too good to be true."

Zoey sighed. "I hope that happens to me," she said.

"You've made a good start with your blog and

your businesses," Daphne praised. "You learn from each success on the way—and from your mistakes. In fact, sometimes you can learn as much from your worst mistakes as you do from your biggest successes."

Zoey wasn't sure she wanted to make too many worst mistakes, even if she did learn a lot from them. Making mistakes was never fun.

After a delicious meal, Daphne took out a small compact and reapplied her lipstick and lip gloss. It was the same brand Fashionsista had sent her as a gift when she was appearing as a guest judge on *Fashion Showdown*.

"I have that exact same lip gloss!" she exclaimed. "I love it! One of my blog readers sent it to me as a present."

"Really?" Daphne said. "I'm not surprised. It's a cult favorite—very popular these days."

Zoey had been saving her Fashionsista lip gloss for special occasions because she wanted it to last for a long time, but now that she knew Daphne Shaw wore it too, she was going to have to save it for *extra* special occasions.

When they returned to the office, Zoey joined Daphne for a meeting in the conference room about the next season's collection. After that, there was another meeting, this time about the status of the current season's production.

"Are you bored?" Daphne asked during a short break.

"No!" Zoey said. "It's all really interesting—even the stuff I'm not sure I understand. I know I'm going to have to learn about it someday if I want to be a fashion designer like you."

"That's true," Daphne said. "But to tell you the truth, after you've been to a few thousand meetings like this, they aren't nearly as interesting as they were in the beginning."

"I can see that," Zoey said. "Like, it was fun making dog outfits a bunch of times, but when I had hundreds of orders to fill, it wasn't so much fun anymore."

"Exactly," Daphne said. "The designing and creative sides of the business are my real loves—but I have to pay attention to the business side too, if I want to be a successful designer."

Before Zoey knew it, it was the end of the day and almost time to meet her dad in the lobby. Back in her office, Daphne kicked off her heels and changed into Converse slip-ons.

"Sorry, Zoey, but my feet are killing me," Daphne said. "Time to switch to Converse for the trip home."

Zoey's eyes widened. "I love Converse too. I was *wondering* how you walked in those heels. They're soooo pretty, but ouch!"

"Ouch is right. Ah, the things we'll do for fashion!" Daphne laughed. "Before you go, I have a little surprise. Something made just for you!" Daphne handed Zoey a small bag. Inside was a note telling Zoey that Daphne hoped she had a wonderful day and to please keep in touch. And, wrapped in silver tissue paper, Zoey found a Daphne Shaw T-shirt in just her size.

Zoey was thrilled. Daphne didn't make a children's line of clothing, and even if she did, most middle-school kids wouldn't be able to afford it!

"Thank you!" Zoey said, giving Daphne a hug. "I love it!"

Zoey found her taxi-shaped bag, which she'd left by Daphne's desk, and rummaged in it until she found a little wrapped gift.

"I've got a present for you, too," she said. "I didn't know your size, so I couldn't make you clothes, so . . ."

Zoey handed Daphne the present, feeling very shy all of a sudden.

"Did you notice I'm wearing one of your designs?" Daphne asked. She took off her blazer, and Zoey realized Daphne was wearing a Tangled top from the Sew Zoey online store.

"Wow!" Zoey exclaimed. "I didn't realize. . . ."

Not only had Daphne bought two dog outfits, she'd also bought a tank top! Zoey couldn't believe Daphne was wearing one of *her* designs.

"This is lovely!" Daphne said, her face lighting up when she saw the fabric necklace Zoey had made for her. "I'm going to put it on right now."

Zoey knew Daphne really did like the necklace and wasn't just pretending because she didn't just take off the necklace she was wearing and put it on; she showed it to everyone they passed on the way to the reception area, where Zoey's dad was waiting.

"Thank you for the most amazing day," Zoey said to Daphne. "I'll never forget it—ever!"

"Thank *you*, Zoey," Daphne said. "I've enjoyed our time together. You've got a wonderful daughter, Mr. Webber," she told Zoey's dad.

"I know," he said, smiling.

"I'm going to take you to Libby's aunt's apartment via the scenic route," Dad said. "That way you'll get a mini-tour of New York."

"Awesome!" Zoey said.

He drove down the West Side Highway, pointing out the Freedom Tower, where the World Trade Center had once stood, and the Statue of Liberty, raising her beacon of light in the middle of New York Harbor. Then he drove up the FDR Drive on the East Side, so Zoey could see the Brooklyn Bridge and the Empire State Building.

Lexie lived on the Upper East Side. When they arrived at her building, they had to drive around the block a few times before finding somewhere to park. Then Dad helped Zoey carry her suitcase up the four flights of stairs to Lexie's apartment.

"Welcome!" Lexie said as they entered what seemed to be her living room and kitchen together, although neither part was very big. A small bedroom opened off from the living room. The colors made Zoey feel like she was in a little jewelry box.

"Whew!" Dad said, catching his breath from the climb. "Cozy place you've got here."

"I love it," Zoey said. "But no wonder you didn't want more than one of us to come with Libby. We would have had to sleep all smushed together! It's tiny!"

Lexie laughed. "Believe it or not, Zoey, this is actually a pretty decent size for an apartment in the city."

Zoey had been really looking forward to moving to New York when she got older, but she'd only ever stayed in a nice hotel with Aunt Lulu. She wondered what it would be like to live in a little apartment like Lexie's.

"Well, I better get going so you ladies can get the party started," Dad said. "I've got a bit of a drive back, and who knows what Marcus is up to. Have a great weekend, girls."

"We will," Libby and Zoey chorused together.

They looked at each other and laughed. Their pajama party weekend had officially begun!

---------- CHAPTER 5 ----------

Fangirl-tastic!

Guess what? I made it through the visit to Daphne Shaw's studio without making a fool of myself! Not only that, it was the best day EVER! Daphne is *sooooo* nice and down-to-earth. I'm not sure why I was scared. I mean, she's a person just like me, right? She was even more fabulous than I hoped she'd be. I'm even more of a fan than I was before!

I got to tour the entire studio and even sit in on some business meetings, which might sound boring, but it wasn't. I'm serious! Even though I didn't understand every single thing they were talking about, I was learning a lot. One thing is definitely for sure: It made me all the more certain that I want to be just like Daphne Shaw when I grow up!

Dad took me on a mini-tour of the city on the way to Libby's aunt's apartment, which is where I got the inspiration for some of today's designs. Can't wait to spend more time exploring the Big Apple!

"Who's up for pancakes?" Lexie asked, drawing the curtains to let daylight into the cramped living room, where Libby and Zoey were sleeping on a blow-up air mattress.

She was still in her pajamas, but they were really stylish ones—blue silk with white polka dots and mother-of-pearl buttons.

"Me." Zoey yawned.

She poked Libby, who was still sleeping.

"What?" Libby asked, half asleep.

"Pancakes?" Zoey asked.

"Uh-huh," Libby said, rubbing the sleep out of her eyes.

Lexie got busy in the kitchen, which was basically in the same room. *It was fun hanging out with her,* Zoey thought—like having a sleepover with their friends, except one of the friends was a grown-up.

"I thought we'd hit the Metropolitan Museum of Art first, then take the subway downtown and go to the Tenement Museum," Lexie said.

"We have to leave time for window-shopping, Aunt Lexie," Libby said.

"And to go to Sweet Sugar Sunshine to get the cupcakes for Priti!" Zoey reminded her.

"Okay, then," Lexie said, "You girls better eat up, because we've got a full day on our plate!"

Zoey had never been to the Metropolitan Museum of Art before and she couldn't believe how big it was.

"Where do you want to start?" Lexie asked. "Ancient? Modern and contemporary?"

"Let Zoey choose," Libby said. "Since it's her first time here."

"Um . . . I can't decide," Zoey said. "I wish I could go to all of them, but I know we don't have time. I guess maybe modern and contemporary?"

"Great choice," Lexie said. "Some of my favorite artists are in those galleries."

Zoey could have happily spent the entire day at the Met with her sketchbook. In fact, she thought, someday she would have to ask her dad if he would bring her back to New York so she could do just that. She was fascinated by how light reflected off of Van Gogh's brushstrokes, how Seurat painted with dots, and how Kandinsky used intense colors. Libby and her aunt had to keep dragging her away from canvases that caught her eye, with the reminder that they had lots more to do that day.

"I feel like my head's about to explode with ideas," Zoey said as they sat on the steps of the museum, enjoying warm, salty, street cart pretzels before heading downtown.

"That's what I love about living in New York," Lexie said. "If you're a creative person, there's so much to inspire you. And not just in museums. Everywhere you look. It's what makes it worth paying crazy rent for a small apartment."

"I definitely want to come here to live someday, maybe for college," Zoey said. "But first, I have to get through middle school!"

"And high school," Libby reminded her.

"Well, let's get moving so we can pack in all the things we have planned," Lexie said. "Like window-shopping."

"YES!" Libby and Zoey chorused together.

"And getting cupcakes," Zoey added. "We can't forget the cupcakes!"

They took the subway down to the Lower East Side. Zoey was glad Libby's aunt knew her way around, because they had to change trains to get to Delancey Street, and Zoey found the subway system really confusing.

"You're in the middle of the Lower East Side now," Aunt Lexie said. "This was the heart of immigrant New York. Imagine the streets crowded with people who'd just come off the boat, all speaking different languages."

"There still are signs in different languages," Zoey said, looking around her at the signs on various storefronts.

"That's because there's still a vibrant immigrant community," Aunt Lexie said. "It's one of the things that makes New York such an interesting place to live."

They walked over to Orchard Street and bought tickets to the Tenement Museum. There, a guide took them on a walking tour of the original tenement building and explained that families lived together in the cramped apartments. They worked long hours under horrible conditions.

Zoey was relieved when they got back outside into the sunshine after the tour was over. The tenement rooms were depressing. They made her appreciate her comfortable room at home—and not having to share it with Marcus *and* Dad!

"It makes my little place seem like a palace, doesn't it?" Lexie asked.

"Yeah, it does. Plus, I can't believe they had to sew in there for fourteen hours a day," Zoey said. "It would take all the fun out of it."

"Young girls in the garment industry worked those kinds of hours, seven days a week," Lexie said.

"You mean kids worked? And they didn't even get the weekend off?" Libby exclaimed.

"We're lucky we live in the United States at a time when children's and workers' rights are protected. In some countries children still work in factories and under horrible conditions," Lexie said, sighing. "But enough sadness. I'm grateful to be here, now, spending the day with you girls. What should we do next?"

"I'm grateful too. But I'm also starving," Libby said.

"Me too," Zoey said.

Lexie laughed.

"Lunch it is. Then we can go up to SoHo and do some window-shopping," Lexie said. "I think we could do with some cheering up. It's always fun to look at all the beautiful things for sale, even if we don't buy them."

The cupcake shop was in the same neighborhood as the Tenement Museum, so Lexie said they would stop there first, before heading to lunch.

"But will the cupcakes be fresh enough if we buy them today?" Zoey asked.

"They should be just fine for a few days, but if you want, I think you can freeze them," Lexie suggested.

"Yay! Sugar Sweet Sunshine, here we come!" Libby said.

"You know what? I'm thinking we should have dessert first today," Lexie suggested. "I can't wait till lunch!"

The following morning, Lexie took the two girls out to brunch at a cute restaurant in her neighborhood. While they were waiting for their food, she told the girls she had a surprise.

"What is it?" Libby asked.

Aunt Lexie rummaged in her handbag and took out an envelope. She handed it to Libby. Inside were three tickets to *Slumberland*, the new musical based on Sleeping Beauty.

"Wow! Thanks, Aunt Lexie!" Libby said. "Mom said it was almost impossible to get tickets for this show!"

Aunt Lexie tapped her nose.

"I have connections," she said, smiling.

"Thank you!" Zoey exclaimed. "I've never been to a Broadway show before!"

"Well, I think you're going to love this one, Zoey," Aunt Lexie said. "The costumes are supposed to be out of this world."

Zoey was so excited, she wasn't sure she'd be able to eat the waffles she'd ordered. But when the waiter put down the plate, her appetite suddenly reappeared. They were so delicious, she finished every last bite.

"I don't think I could eat another crumb," Aunt Lexie said after they'd finished. "How about we walk across Central Park to the theater, to stretch our legs?"

It was a beautiful day; warm and sunny, but not humid. They walked west from Lexie's neighborhood and crossed Park Avenue, waving at the doormen who guarded the entrances of each of the imposing apartment buildings.

"Look! There's a dog wearing one of your Doggie Duds outfits!" Libby said.

Sure enough, Zoey saw a fashionably dressed woman walking a dog wearing the Draper. She couldn't believe one of her dog outfits was being worn on Park Avenue!

"I can't believe people get so dressed up on the weekend," Zoey said. "She looked like she just walked off the cover of *Très Chic!*"

Aunt Lexie laughed. "New York is the city that never sleeps, Zoey. I guess that goes for the fashionistas too."

Having to be fashionable 24/7 sounds tiring, Zoey thought. She loved to dress well, but once in a while it was fun to just be a slob.

Lexie made sure they strolled down Madison Avenue for a few blocks, so they could check out the windows of the boutiques.

"Madison Avenue is one of my favorite places to window-shop," Lexie said.

Zoey wished she had her sketch pad with her— but as it turned out, they didn't really have time for sketching. Lexie made them keep up a brisk pace across Fifth Avenue to Central Park.

It seemed to Zoey like the warm weather had brought half of New York to Central Park. There were people everywhere she looked—playing soccer, roller-skating, bike riding, playing Frisbee, dancing, sitting on the grass and reading a book.

"Sometimes I like to come here, sit on a bench, and just people watch," Lexie confessed. "You see all kinds of characters."

Zoey decided that she would have to come back to New York and do some people watching in Central Park. She bet her sketchbook would be filled with interesting ideas after a few hours of watching New Yorkers walk by.

When they exited on the west side of the park, they continued over to Broadway.

"Broadway! Don't you just want to dance and sing?" Libby asked, skipping a few steps and pretending to tap dance.

"Um . . . ," Zoey said. But then she laughed and started to pretend to tap dance along with Libby.

Lexie shook her head, smiling. "Where do you

two get the energy? My feet are killing me from the walk across the park!"

"Come on, Aunt Lexie! You're not *that* old!" Libby said, linking her arm through her aunt's as well as Zoey's.

"If you can't beat them, join them," Lexie said, and she pretended to tap dance down the sidewalk with Zoey and Libby.

By the time they got to the theater, they were all out of breath. Zoey took her *Playbill* from the usher and gazed up at the elaborate patterns on the ceiling of the theater as they were led to their seats.

"Careful, Zo. You almost tripped on that old lady's cane!" Lexie warned.

"Oops, sorry," Zoey said. "It's just so . . . beautiful here."

"I know. I love these old theaters," Aunt Lexie said. "But it might be a little safer to look at the ceiling when we're sitting down."

Zoey loved everything about the theater—from the red velvet chairs to the huge chandelier hanging above their heads to the thick red velvet curtain across the stage. When the lights dimmed and the music started, she almost clapped her hands in excitement—except that no one else was clapping yet, so she didn't.

And then the overture ended and the curtain opened on a fairy tale castle, where cooks were preparing the feast to celebrate the birth of baby Aurora. Zoey was transported. The sets were amazing. The singing was fantastic. And the costumes! It must have been so much fun to be the costume designer for *Slumberland*—to design all those beautiful outfits for the lords and ladies of the court, for the fairies, and for Aurora.

"What do you think?" Aunt Lexie asked when the red velvet curtain closed for intermission, right after Aurora pricked her finger on the spindle and the whole castle fell into an enchanted sleep.

"I love the dancing," Libby said. "And the singing."

"You were right—the costumes *are* amazing!" Zoey said. "And the sets! The whole thing. Thank you so much for taking me."

"It's my pleasure," Lexie said. "Now, who wants some peanut M&M's?"

The second half was even better than the first. Zoey couldn't believe how quickly they changed the set for each scene. It was one thing in the movies, where they could film in different locations and use special effects, but this was right in front her very eyes—and the eyes of an entire theater audience!

When the final curtain came down, the audience rose for a standing ovation, and Zoey, Libby, and Lexie were on their feet, cheering loudly and clapping.

"We better take a taxi home," Lexie said when they emerged from the theater. "I don't want to keep Libby's mom waiting when she comes to pick you girls up—especially since you have a long drive back. Of course, *getting* a taxi when all the matinees let out is another story. . . ."

They had to walk for about five blocks before they finally got a taxi, and they arrived back at Lexie's apartment just as Libby's mom got there.

"Perfect timing, sis," Lexie said.

"How was your weekend, girls?" Mrs. Flynn asked.

"Amazing!" Zoey said.

"Fun!" Libby agreed.

"Thank you so much for having me," Zoey told Lexie.

"Anytime," Lexie told her. "I hope you and Libby will come back to visit again soon."

Zoey couldn't wait to take Lexie up on her offer. New York was definitely her favorite place in the whole world. Well, except for home, where Dad and Marcus were waiting.

------------ CHAPTER 6 ------------

The Fine Art of Fashion

New York is the most amazing place—I definitely want to live there when I grow up. But right now it's kind of a relief to be back in quiet little Mapleton after such a whirlwind weekend. My head is still spinning from everything I saw and experienced at Daphne

Shaw's studio (*thank you*, Daphne!!) and going to all the museums with Libby and her aunt. Oh! And seeing my very first Broadway musical, which was just . . . MAGICAL. (*Thank you*, Lexie!!) I can't wait to spend some time sketching all the ideas I've got in my head and doing some sewing. I'll be sure to keep you posted!

Zoey was exhausted when Mrs. Flynn dropped her—and Priti's cupcakes—at home. After a good night's sleep in her own bed, she couldn't wait to catch up with Priti and give her the sweet treats. Kate was already away at soccer camp, but Zoey, Libby, and Priti arranged to meet at the pool the next day to share news. Marcus was lifeguarding at the pool for the summer again and offered to give Zoey a ride.

"Make sure you drive really carefully," she said after she buckled her seat belt. "The cupcakes I'm bringing for Priti are on the backseat."

"I *always* drive carefully," Marcus said. "I am an expert chauffeur."

Marcus was a good driver, but Dad had always

told them they had to watch out for the *other* drivers on the road. Sure enough, when they were almost at the pool, the car in front of them stopped unexpectedly. Marcus had to slam on the brakes hard, sending the box of cupcakes flying off the backseat and onto the floor of the car.

"Oh no!" Zoey cried. "Priti's cupcakes!"

Thankfully, the box stayed closed. When they parked the car in the pool's parking lot, Zoey picked up the box to inspect it. She was afraid to look inside. Slowly, she opened the lid.

"They look awful," Zoey wailed. "How can I give them to Priti now?"

"I'm sure they still taste just as good," Marcus said. "I'd be happy to eat one, just to make sure."

"You just want a cupcake," Zoey said.

"Well, *duh!*" Marcus said.

"Okay," Zoey said, handing him one. "But only because this one is really messed up."

"Schtill dewishous," Marcus said through a mouthful of cupcake.

"Ew!" Zoey said. "Didn't Dad ever tell you not to talk with your mouth full?"

"Sowwy," Marcus said.

Zoey shut the lid of the box and licked the icing off her fingers. She had to admit Marcus was right—they were "schtill dewishous"!

Priti was just as easygoing about the cupcakes.

"There's frosting and there's cake—what's not to like?" she asked. "It's all going to end up in my tummy anyway, right?"

"Right," Libby said, taking a cupcake for herself.

When they each had one, they "clinked" them together, as if doing a toast and just like they do with ice cream cones.

"To summer adventures," Priti said.

"Definitely!" Zoey agreed.

"I'm starting ballet camp next Monday," Libby said. "That's going to be adventure, for sure."

"I want to hear all about Zoey's adventures with Daphne Shaw," Priti said.

"Oh my gosh, it was *amazing*," Zoey said. "She showed me all around her studio, and then she took me out to lunch, and then I got to go to meetings. And then she gave me a T-shirt from her collection. It was the perfect day!"

"Wow." Priti sighed. "It must have been."

"But we're going to have a lot of perfect days this summer, aren't we, Priti?" Zoey said. "Did you hear we're going to summer camp together?"

"Yes!" Priti said. "My parents told me. I'm so excited!"

"Wait—where are you guys going?" Libby asked.

"It's called Blue Mountain Camp for the Arts," Priti said. "I wasn't that worried about making new friends, but having one of my besties with me will make it easier to be away from home for so long. Besides, everything is more fun with Zoey there."

"It sounds great," Libby said. "You have to promise to write to me!"

"We will," Zoey said.

"I'm just glad my parents are going to use the time to take a romantic trip. You know, like a second honeymoon," Priti said. "Maybe it's just what they need to remember how much they're in love with each other, so when I get back, they'll have one of those renewal of vows ceremonies. Then Tara and Sashi and I can be bridesmaids!"

"And Zoey can design your bridesmaid dresses!" Libby suggested.

Nothing would make Zoey happier than to design bridesmaid dresses for the Holbrooke girls, especially if it meant their parents were getting along better. Priti had been worrying about her parents getting divorced for a while now. Even though her friend was, by nature, a happy, optimistic person, Zoey could tell that it was starting to get her down. She would have to keep her fingers *and* her toes crossed that everything worked out for the best.

The next day, Zoey was in her room, packing for camp, when Marcus knocked on the door.

"Come in!" she called.

Her brother plopped himself onto the bed and surveyed the piles of clothes she was getting ready to put into her trunk.

"You're not going to need any of that fashionable, frilly stuff at camp," he said.

"This isn't regular camp," Zoey said. "It's arts camp."

"I know," Marcus said. "But my friend Mikey went to that same camp, and he said they wear uniforms."

"*Uniforms?*" Zoey exclaimed. "No way! No one said anything to me about *uniforms*! I just escaped from the uniform curse this year."

She stomped to the door. "I'm going to ask Dad."

Marcus followed her downstairs to where their father was sitting in the living room, watching TV and working on his laptop.

"Dad, Marcus said Blue Mountain Camp for the Arts makes campers wear uniforms," she said. "Is that true?"

"I don't remember Mr. Holbrooke saying anything about that, but let me check," Dad said.

He went on to the camp website and found the camp policies section.

"Oh boy. . . . Yes, it does look like there's a uniform policy," he said. "I'm sorry, honey, I didn't realize."

Seeing Zoey's mutinous expression, he added, "But it's probably just as well, because that way you won't ruin your nice clothes."

"But, *Daaaad*," Zoey complained. "I only just got out of uniforms. This is like taking a step backward."

"It's only for six weeks, Zo," Marcus reasoned. "You can handle it. What doesn't kill you makes you stronger and all that."

Zoey glared at her brother. She didn't *want* to handle it. She wanted to wear her own clothes.

"I'd better check what other rules they have while we're at it," Dad said. He scanned the web page for a minute. "Uh-oh . . ."

"What?" Zoey asked. "Uh-oh" didn't sound good. Not good at all.

"There's a strict *no technology* rule," Dad said. "No cell phones. No computers."

"No way!" Zoey wailed. "How am I supposed to go six weeks without blogging? I have readers! They expect regular posts!"

"Look, before you get too upset, let me talk to the camp director and see if she can make an exception, given that you have a well-established and popular blog with a big following," her father said. "If not, maybe you can send me your posts in letters, and I'll post them for you."

"Or you could write some posts in advance and preschedule them," Marcus suggested.

"It's not the same," Zoey grumbled.

"Let's just wait and see what she says, okay?" Dad said.

"What about my sewing machine?" Zoey said. "I can't go a whole summer without sewing."

"I'll ask about that, too," Dad said. "Don't worry, Zo. It's going to be okay. You know, honey, a little time in the great outdoors might be good for you."

"Yeah. Mikey said it was a great camp," Marcus said. "He loved it there."

Zoey put on a brave face, but she wasn't feeling at all happy about going anymore. Uniforms aside, how was she going to survive six weeks without blogging?

The next evening at dinner, her father said he'd spoken to the camp director.

"The good news is that she was really impressed to hear you'd built up such a popular blog and to hear about your appearance as a judge on *Fashion Showdown*. She's very excited to have you as a camper."

"But what's the bad news?" Zoey asked, afraid to hear the answer.

"Well, they're very strict about the no technology rule, and they can't make any exceptions, not even for you," he said. "I'm sorry, Zo. But she also said she thinks you'll be having so much fun, you won't even miss blogging."

Zoey couldn't imagine how it was possible to have *that* much fun. It was going to be a long six weeks.

"Wait—what did she say about my sewing machine?"

Her father grimaced.

"I'm afraid that's a no-go too."

"But sewing is my art!" Zoey argued. "How can I go to an art camp without my sewing machine?"

"I explained that," her dad said. "The director said there's at least one sewing machine at the camp—in the theater department. Maybe you can help with the costumes."

"I guess." Zoey sighed. "But I'm going to pack my new pincushion that Fashionsista sent, and some colored threads and needles and some fabrics, just in case I get stir-crazy and need to sew by hand, old-school style."

"That's my girl," her dad said. "Adapt and make the best of it. And you know what? I have a feeling you'll end up having a really great time."

"Mikey did," Marcus said. "He didn't even care about the uniform much."

"But he's a *guy*," Zoey pointed out. "It's not the same."

Still, she hoped her dad, Marcus, and Mikey were right and that she would end up having a good time. She wished she felt as confident about it as everyone else.

---------- CHAPTER 7 ----------

Camp Hiatus

I've got good news and bad news. The good news is that Priti and I are going to camp together! It's not called Camp Hiatus, though—which brings me to the bad news. The camp doesn't allow laptops and other technology, so Sew Zoey is going to have to be on hiatus while I'm there. ☹ Unfortunately, there are no exceptions, not even for fashion bloggers!

And there's another rule I'm not so crazy about either: We have to wear uniforms. Ugh. I thought I was done with all that when Ms. Austen scrapped the uniform code at Mapleton Prep. I'm hoping that maybe being stuck wearing a uniform again for six weeks will make me superinspired to design more fabulous clothes when I get back. Maybe if I say that enough, I'll believe it. In the meantime, I've drawn a dress to get me in the mood to start roughing it. I imagine this tent-shaped dress being made of waterproof material, like a real tent. Perfect for rain or shine!

So this is my last post for a while . . . but according to my dad, I'll be back before I know it. See you in six weeks! TTFN, xo, Zoey

When Aunt Lulu came for dinner the night before Zoey left for camp, she and Buttons brought a gift. Dad made Zoey wait until after they'd eaten and cleaned up all the dishes before she could open it. The suspense was killing her!

"It's actually a joint gift from your dad and me," Aunt Lulu said.

"But I let Aunt Lulu do the choosing, because she's got better taste," Dad explained.

"Wise move, Dad," Marcus said.

Zoey unwrapped a pretty decoupage box filled with fun stationery, envelopes, cool stickers, and postage stamps, so she could write letters home and to her friends about her camp experiences. Aunt Lulu had also bought her a pretty journal to write and draw in, and a set of colored gel pens and some sketching pencils.

"Thank you!" Zoey said. "I love the box. And the stationery is so cute!"

"We figured you could kick it old-school, like we did when we went to camp," Aunt Lulu said. "Getting to pick our camp stationery was part of the fun."

"Make sure you write at least once a week, okay?" Dad said. "'Cause I'll miss having you around."

"I will," Zoey said. "I'll miss you all, too. And wearing my own clothes. And my sewing machine and my computer and my phone."

"I bet Zoey will miss her computer more than she'll miss me," Marcus joked.

"No, not my computer. But I'll definitely miss *Buttons* more," Zoey said, picking up the dog and cuddling him. The dog licked her ear and her forehead.

Aunt Lulu and Dad laughed.

Zoey just hoped she didn't get homesick. She'd never been to sleepaway camp before. She'd never really been away from home for more than a week or so. Just thinking about it made her feel jittery.

The following morning, Mr. and Mrs. Holbrooke dropped off Priti and helped load all her camp gear into Mr. Webber's car. By the time both girls' trunks were loaded, there wasn't much room left over!

They had a cozy ride up to camp, playing I Spy, singing songs, and imagining what camp would be like.

When they arrived, Dad helped them unload the trunks and then waited until they were assigned to their cabins. They were in different cabins, which made Zoey a little nervous, but Priti assured her they could meet for lunch and different activities.

"I'll say good-bye, then," Dad said. "Have a great time and don't forget to write!"

Zoey hugged her father tight.

"I'll miss you, Dad."

Dad ruffled her hair. "You'll be too busy having fun to miss your old dad much, Zo. See you soon, honey." He gave Zoey one more hug and then got into the car to drive back home.

"Are you Zoey?" asked a counselor in a golf cart.

When Zoey nodded, she said, "I'm Brooke, the counselor in charge of your cabin. Help me load your trunk onto the back, and I'll give you a ride up."

"Zoey, let's meet after we unpack!" Priti called. She was already heading up the path in another golf cart with her bunk counselor.

"Is this your first time at sleepaway camp?" Brooke asked.

"Yes," Zoey admitted. "Is it that obvious?"

Brooke smiled. "You have that deer-in-the-headlights look," she said. "But don't worry. We've got a great group of girls in our bunk. You're going to have a blast."

It sounded like the campers in her cabin were *already* having a blast when Brooke helped her unload her trunk from the golf cart and then carry it inside.

"Hey, everyone, this is Zoey," Brooke said.

"Hey, Zoey!" called a girl from the top bunk at the end of the cabin. "I'm Marisol."

"And I'm Kelly," said a red-haired girl with freckles. "Welcome to the best cabin at Blue Mountain!"

After a bunch of hellos, there was one more girl to meet.

"Hi," said a girl with her blond hair in a perfect French braid and fire-engine red sneakers. "I'm Campbell."

"Hi," Zoey said. "I love your sneakers!"

"Thanks," Campbell said, her face lighting up with a smile. "Got to wear something to brighten up these uniforms."

"I know what you mean," Zoey said.

As Zoey unpacked her trunk and changed into her uniform, the girls chatted about where they were from and their previous camp experiences.

"Don't worry about being a camp newbie," Marisol told her. "It's really fun here."

"Yeah, that's what my brother's friend said," Zoey replied. "And besides, my friend Priti is here too, but she's in another cabin. We're meeting up after I unpack and change."

"I love your outfit," Kelly said, eyeing Zoey's daisy-print top and denim shorts, which she'd embroidered with daisies to match. "Bet you're *thrilled* about the uniform, huh?

"Not so much," Zoey said with a sigh, holding up the hated shorts and shirt at arm's length as she removed them from her trunk.

"You'll get used to it," Marisol said. "And you'll have so much fun, you won't even care what you're wearing!"

When Zoey changed into her uniform and looked at herself in the mirror in the cabin bathroom, she wasn't sure if *that* much fun was even possible.

"So what are you going to do first?" Priti asked when they met up on the path between their cabins. "I'm thinking of taking songwriting and canoeing."

"Oh," Zoey said. She really wanted to do arts and crafts, and the nature walk.

"What?" Priti searched Zoey's face. "You don't have to do the same things as me if you don't want to, Zo. It's okay. We can meet at lunch."

"Are you sure?" Zoey asked.

"Totally. That way we can both meet new friends and introduce them to one another," Priti said.

"Sounds like a plan!" Zoey said. "Have fun!"

They went off in their separate directions. Zoey had a great morning on the nature walk. The counselor pointed out a scarlet tanager and a yellow-bellied sapsucker, and Zoey picked up some pinecones and acorns that gave her ideas for new designs. She couldn't wait to get back to her cabin and sketch. But first it was time for lunch, and Zoey was starving after her time in the great outdoors.

Her plans to have lunch with Priti were foiled by Brooke, who told her that for lunch, they had to eat with their bunkmates, as a bonding exercise. Zoey wondered if she was really helping Priti at all since they weren't doing the same activities and couldn't even eat together. But when she spotted her friend across the cafeteria, she seemed to be having a good time chatting with the girls from her cabin. Zoey got a burrito and went to sit with the girls from her own bunk. She liked the girls, but the burrito . . . not so much. But then Brooke made up for her burrito blues by handing her a letter from Marcus. He must have mailed it before she even left for camp!

Zoey read the letter on her way to arts and crafts:

Dear Zoey,

Hey! How are the creepy-crawlies treating you? Hope you're surviving life back in uniform and with NO COMPUTER! *Shock, horror*

Life here at Casa Webber is pretty much the same as usual. Allie says hi! Yes, we're still a thing, in case you're wondering.

Any cute guy campers at Blue Mountain Camp? (Don't worry, I won't tell Dad—if you pay me enough to keep my mouth shut! ☺)

Aunt Lulu and Buttons say hi and woof!

Xo,

Marcus

Zoey stuffed the letter into her pocket. It made her miss Marcus. And home. Luckily, when she walked into arts and crafts, she saw a sort-of familiar face—Campbell, the sweet girl from her cabin with the bright red sneakers. She waved Zoey over to sit at the same table.

"Hey, are you okay?" Campbell asked.

"I just got a letter from my brother," Zoey confessed. "It made me homesick, and I only just got here!"

"This is your first time at sleepaway camp, right?"

Zoey nodded.

"Don't worry. Lots of people get homesick at first. It'll get easier."

The girls chatted away as they painted. Campbell was a bit quiet at first, but soon she became really animated. Zoey was having so much fun talking that she accidentally spilled paint on her pants.

"Maybe this uniform thing isn't such a bad idea after all," she muttered.

"Yeah," Campbell said. "Stuff gets really gross after six weeks in the woods. It's better if it doesn't happen to your clothes!"

After the crafts session, the two walked to dinner together.

"I hope dinner is better than lunch," Zoey said. "My burrito was pretty barf-worthy."

"I didn't think it was *that* bad," Campbell said. "I kind of liked it, actually. Maybe I was just really hungry?"

"Oh, sorry! Well, I think I'm going to get cereal for dinner," Zoey said, "just to be safe."

She went over to the cereal bar, which was offered as an option at every meal. After pouring herself a heaping bowl, she looked around for Priti, who she'd promised to meet for dinner. She spotted her . . . sitting next to Campbell!

How did Campbell and Priti know each other? And wasn't she just talking to Campbell in the food line? How did she manage to sit down so fast?

Zoey turned around, and to her disbelief, Campbell was walking toward her with a tray.

"Where do you want to sit?" Campbell asked.

"Wait . . . ," Zoey said, looking back over at Priti and the *other* Campbell. "Um . . . I think I'm starting to see things. Because my friend Priti is sitting over there . . . with someone who *looks like your clone!*"

Campbell started laughing.

"You're not seeing things, and she's not a clone. She's my twin sister, Taylor. C'mon, I'll introduce you."

They walked over to where Priti and Taylor were sitting.

"Hey, Priti!" Zoey said, and then turned to Campbell. "Priti is my BFF from home."

"Hi, Zo," Priti said when she looked up from her plate . . . and then she saw Campbell. "Whaaaaa?"

She looked back and forth, from Campbell to Taylor and back again.

"I think I have sunstroke from canoeing all day," she said. "I'm seeing double!"

"No, you're not! We're twins!" Taylor said.

"Identical twins," added Campbell.

"OMG, you—you're like carbon copies," Priti said, shaking her head. "You guys even have matching French braids . . . and the same red sneakers. WOW."

Zoey and Campbell sat down to join the other two girls.

"Sorry," Taylor said. "We didn't mean to freak you out, really."

"Yeah," Campbell added. "It's just that we wanted to spend the first day at camp being ourselves first and then twins second, because we never get a chance to do that. We had no idea we'd end up making friends with two girls who were already friends!"

"We're like BFF twins!" Priti said.

"Well, except that we don't look anything alike," added Zoey, scooping up a spoonful of cereal.

"So . . . I have to ask. Zoey, why are you having cereal for dinner?" Taylor asked.

"Well, I didn't love the burrito at lunch," Zoey explained. "But mostly because my dad's really into health food, so I don't eat sugary cereal at home. It's so good, I might just have to eat it for every meal for the entire six weeks!"

"Warning, everyone! We might have to stage a *cereal*vention," Priti announced. "We don't want Zoey to go home from camp with dentures because all her teeth have fallen out from eating all that sugar!"

"Don't worry, Priti, I'm only joking," Zoey said. "Well, *half* joking."

After dinner, the girls headed out to the camp's kickoff bonfire down by the lake. Priti was the first to spot the picnic tables, where trays were piled high with graham crackers, marshmallows, and chocolate bars.

"S'mores!" Priti exclaimed. "This camp just gets better and better!"

They feasted on s'mores, sang songs, and looked for constellations in the darkened sky above the treetops. By the time they made their way back to their cabins, the four girls were already fast friends.

---------- CHAPTER 8 ----------

Pining Over Pinecones

Dear Dad and Marcus,

I'm having a great time—in spite of the bug bites and burritos! Even though Priti and I aren't in the same bunk, we've both made new friends, and guess what? They're identical twins!! Not only that, in their uniforms, it's impossible to tell them apart, especially since they wear their hair the same way and have the same bright red sneakers, too, so it can get pretty confusing. The sketch is inspired by the nature walk we took yesterday. The pinecones and tree rings were so beautiful. They almost made me forget to miss my cell phone! Almost, but not quite . . . Don't worry Dad, I'm getting lots of fresh air. I'm turning into a regular outdoorsy girl, which is great except for all the mosquito bites. Thanks for reminding me to pack the anti-itch stuff. You rock! ☺ Even though I'm having fun, I miss you guys—especially your cooking, Dad. The food here is kind of yuck. I think you can send care packages, though (hint! hint!).

Xoxo,
Zoey

"So, are you guys going to try out with me for the play?" Priti asked at lunch the next day. "It's *A Midsummer Night's Dream*. You know, Shakespeare? It's about all these star-crossed lovers in a wood. There are nobles and kings and queens and fairies. Oh, and a guy called Bottom who gets turned into a donkey."

"Wait? There's a guy whose name is . . . Bottom?" Campbell said. "As in, like, you know . . ."

"Butt?" added Taylor.

Priti giggled. She told Zoey, "Tara and Sashi said there're all kinds of funny stuff in Shakespeare's plays, if you can get over the Old English-y way of talking." Then, turning to Campbell and Taylor, she added, "My sisters are twins too, but they're not identical. Actually, they couldn't be more different from each other, and me. They wouldn't dream of acting!"

"I'm not really an onstage kind of girl, either," Zoey said. "That's more your thing than mine, Priti."

"Me neither," Campbell said.

"I like singing, so maybe I'd like acting, too. I wouldn't mind auditioning if it means we get to hang out," Taylor said. "But I don't know if I want a big part."

"Okay! Zoey . . . Campbell . . . you have to try out too!" Priti urged them. "We can all practice our lines together and chill at rehearsals and talk to"—she lowered her voice—*"boys!"*

Even though talking to boys wasn't high on Zoey's list of things to do at camp, it was hard to resist Priti's enthusiasm.

"Okay, I'll do it," Zoey said.

"Me too!" Taylor added.

"Well," Campbell said, "maybe I can work on set decorations instead of auditioning?"

"Totally!" Priti exclaimed. "Yay! This is going to be so much fun!"

At Priti's suggestion, the girls practiced their lines together. Zoey found the Shakespearean English really hard to memorize, and she kept flubbing her audition piece. Campbell, though, was incredible. She seemed to have memorized the entire play flawlessly in no time, even though she wasn't auditioning.

"How did you *do* that?" Zoey asked after Campbell helped her with a line she'd messed up for the fifth time.

Campbell shrugged. "I guess I have a . . . kind of . . . photographic memory," she said. "It comes in handy for stuff like this."

"I wish I had a photographic memory," Priti said wistfully. "I really want to be cast as Titania, but she has so many lines."

"Let's do everyone's audition scenes a few more times," Campbell said. "I can't teach you how to have a photographic memory, but I can try to help you learn your lines."

"I can't believe it!" Priti croaked at breakfast the next morning.

It was the morning of auditions for the camp theater production, and she sounded as if she'd swallowed a frog.

"Why do I have to wake up with a cold *today, of all days*!" she wailed dramatically. Well, wailed as much as her scratchy throat and stuffy nose would let her. "It's the most *important day of my life!*"

"Mom tells us to gargle warm salt water when we have a sore throat," Taylor suggested. "It sounds gross, but it helps."

"Dad makes me hot tea with honey and lemon," Zoey said. "I'll go get you some."

"That's okay, Zo," Priti rasped. "I'll go gargle with warm salt water in the bathroom."

Zoey went to get the tea anyway, and by the time she got back with a steaming mug of chamomile with lemon and honey, Priti had gargled an entire mug of warm salt water.

"Do you feel any better?" Campbell asked.

"It soothed my throat a little, but I still sound terrible." Priti groaned.

She *did* sound terrible.

"Here, try drinking the tea," Zoey said.

Even after a few sips, Priti still sounded very froggy. But like a true thespian, she vowed to perform the best she could, anyway.

"The show must go on!" she squawked.

There were more campers than Zoey expected in the theater for auditions.

"Wow, I never thought doing the play would be so popular," she said.

Priti nudged her and then pointed to a good-looking boy. "See! Didn't I tell you there would be cute boys here?"

The boy certainly *was* cute, but Zoey was more concerned with the auditions.

"Break a leg, Priti!" Zoey laughed. "And good luck with the cute boy, too!"

The boy's name turned out to be Nick, and he aced his audition. Zoey was pretty sure he was going to get a lead.

Priti lived up to her promise to do the best she could, in spite of her voice.

"'What angel awakes me from my flowery bed?'" she croaked, pretending to stretch and yawn as if she just woken up.

"Priti's got so much personality," Taylor whispered. "She's great onstage!"

"I know," Zoey whispered back. "But it's hard to hear her because of her sore throat."

Taylor and Zoey went backstage to get ready for their turns. Zoey was nervous but excited to try out. Taylor was visibly shaky, having never auditioned for a play before. Campbell hugged Taylor, then eyed her worriedly when Taylor was called to center stage.

Campbell whispered to Zoey that her sister secretly envied Priti's comfort level onstage. Both twins were on the quiet side, but while Campbell dreamed about writing a book one day or becoming an artist, Taylor loved singing in the school choir and dreamed of being a star.

Taylor's voice wasn't big and showstopping, but it was beautiful. Since this was a play and not a musical, though, it wasn't much help.

"I hope she gets a good part," Zoey said. "Fingers crossed!"

But being center stage, with all eyes upon her, seemed to make Taylor's mind go completely blank. She opened her mouth, but nothing came out. She glanced over at the wings, where Campbell and Zoey were standing, a panicked expression on her face.

That's when Campbell called out the first few lines.

"'O, I am out of breath in this fond chase! The more my prayer, the lesser is my grace,'" Campbell said softly from the wings.

Taylor's face lit up. Zoey could almost see Taylor's memory come back and click in. Taylor repeated the lines Campbell had given her and then continued flawlessly:

"'Happy is Hermia, wheresoe'er she lies;
For she hath blessed and attractive eyes.
How came her eyes so bright? Not with
salt tears:
If so, my eyes are oftener wash'd than
hers.'"

When she came offstage after finishing her monologue, she hugged her sister. "Thanks for helping me out," she said. "I couldn't remember the first line for anything! I totally choked."

Zoey was getting more and more nervous about trying out. She wished she'd never let Priti talk her into this.

"Zoey Webber. You're up!" the director called.

"Well, here goes nothing," Zoey said. She'd picked a short piece of Hippolyta's dialogue to memorize, because she found Shakespeare so hard.

"'I was with Hercules and Cadmus once,
When in a wood of Crete they bay'd the bear
With hounds of Sparta . . .' and . . . um . . .'"

Zoey froze. *What's the next line?* she thought.

Luckily for Zoey, Campbell was offstage to prompt her.

"'Never did I hear such gallant chiding . . . ,'" Campbell said in a loud stage whisper.

It was enough to jog Zoey's memory, and she got through the rest of her audition piece.

"Who is the mysterious person backstage who seems to know the play backward and forward?" Ms. Natasha, the director, asked.

Campbell popped her head out sheepishly from behind the side curtain.

"Um . . . it's me. Campbell."

"When are you auditioning?" Ms. Natasha asked, checking the list on her clipboard. "I don't see anyone named Campbell on the sign-up sheet. Oh wait, you look . . . Weren't you just onstage? Didn't you just audition?"

"No, that was my twin, Taylor. I wasn't planning to audition," Campbell said. "I want to do set design."

"I'd like to see what you can do since you already know the lines," the director said. "Why don't you come on out and give it a try?"

"It's really not my thing," Campbell demurred.

"Humor me," the director replied.

Campbell slouched out to center stage. "Which scene do you want me to do?" she asked.

"Pick a scene, any scene," the director said. "You seem to know all of them!"

"O-Okay," Campbell said.

Then she ran through Titania's monologue, the one she'd spent so much time helping Priti to learn. Zoey was impressed. The sometimes-quiet Campbell was captivating. Even from backstage, Zoey could see the director scribbling notes furiously onto her clipboard.

After the auditions, the girls wanted to talk about anything but the auditions. They hadn't gone as planned for any of the four friends, so it had all been a bit of a letdown—especially for Priti, who had the highest hopes for a big part.

"I really want the lead even more now," she confessed to Zoey privately. "I'm sure Nick's going to get a lead, and if I get one too, then we have to spend more time together. And some of the lead parts even get to *kiss*!"

"You have great stage presence," Zoey said. "I'm sure Ms. Natasha could see that, even if your voice was a little croaky."

"I hope so," Priti said. "I just hate having to wait and see!"

------------ CHAPTER 9 ------------

Bugging Out

Dear Aunt Lulu and Buttons,

Greetings from the great outdoors. Nature is really beautiful, except I'm not sure why there has to be so many insects— especially mosquitoes. I've sketched some imaginary outfits I would want to make for you if you came to visit. Basically, you'd be wrapped in mosquito netting from head to toe! I remembered you said insect prints are really popular in interior design, so I bet they'd make cool clothes, too.

Anyway, Priti and my new identical-twin friends, Campbell and Taylor, joke that the mosquitoes like me best because I'm so sweet—which just makes me want to do something mean to make the mosquitoes not bite me so much! Just kidding—but I do itch a LOT!! Priti's scratching, but for a different reason—she can't wait for the cast list to go up for *A Midsummer Night's Dream*, so she can see if she got a leading role—especially one where kissing might be involved. To keep her from going crazy in the meantime, I've been trying to distract her with a different kind of kiss— the Hershey's Kisses you sent in the care package. Thank you!! I miss you both—give Buttons an extra treat from me.

Xoxo,

Zoey

A few days later, the girls were almost done with lunch when Marisol mentioned that the cast list had been posted. Priti immediately said, "I'm finished," took her tray up to the return, and raced off to the theater department.

"I'm going to go too," Zoey said, getting up and taking her tray. "I want to be there to congratulate Priti."

"Me too," Taylor said.

"I'll follow you in a sec," Campbell said. "I want to grab another cookie."

There was a big crowd around the cast list when Zoey and Taylor got there. They couldn't get close enough to see it, and they couldn't see Priti. But then she emerged from the fray, strangely subdued— not at all her usual, exuberant self—and for once, speechless.

"What happened?" Zoey asked. "Are you okay?"

Priti just shrugged and then walked away.

Zoey gave Taylor a worried look, and they both wormed their way to the front of the crowd to look at the cast list. Zoey couldn't believe her eyes. The name next to the leading role that Priti wanted so badly was . . . *Campbell*, with Taylor as her understudy.

Priti had been cast as Puck, which was a fun supporting role, but Puck didn't get to kiss Oberon—who was going to be played by the very cute Nick.

Taylor was in the Company, and Zoey was listed as the costume designer, but with a question mark after her name and a note to go speak to the director.

"Oh no!" Taylor said. "Priti must be so upset! It's not like Campbell even planned on auditioning until the director made her do it."

"I know!" Zoey said. "Let's go find Priti. She's going to need some serious cheering up."

Priti was sitting on a bench just inside the doors of the drama building, looking very glum. Just as

Zoey and Taylor found her, Campbell walked by. As soon as the crowd around the cast list spotted her, they all started cheering, much to Campbell's confusion.

"What's going on?" she asked her friends.

Zoey and Taylor glanced at Priti, who was staring at a spot on the floor, apparently trying to avoid looking at Campbell at all costs.

"Um . . . well . . . it seems like you got the lead," Zoey explained. "You've been cast as Titania."

"*What?*" Campbell exclaimed. "But . . . what about Priti? I didn't even *want* to audition!"

Priti was quieter than Zoey had ever seen her.

"I . . . I'm happy for you, Campbell," Priti said, her voice cracking. "I don't want to be a crybaby or anything. It's just disappointed not to get my first choice part, is all." She sighed heavily. "I think I just need a little time alone. I'll . . . see you guys later."

"Okay, Priti. See you later," Zoey said, her brow creased with worry for her friend. She knew that not getting the chance to kiss Nick, her crush, was just doubling Priti's disappointment.

"We have to do something," Campbell said as

she watched Priti walk away with her shoulders slumped and her feet dragging. "This is so wrong."

"But what can we do?" Taylor asked. "It's not our decision."

"We can talk to the director," Zoey suggested. "I have to talk to her anyway, about the costume thing. I didn't think they'd need a costume designer, to be honest. I thought they'd already have costumes or they'd rent them."

"Let's do it," Campbell said. "Right now."

They headed straight to the theater director's office and asked if they could speak to her.

"Sure," she said. "What's on your mind?"

Campbell explained her dilemma and asked if Priti could have her role instead.

"Here's the thing, girls," Ms. Natasha said. "I need someone with a big voice and a strong personality to play the role of Puck, and even with a bad cold, I could tell Priti was my girl. She just radiates personality. Puck is a great role for her—it's actually more challenging and interesting than Titania."

She looked from Campbell to Taylor and then back to Campbell.

"I'm sorry, which one of you is which? I'm embarrassed to say I can't tell."

"I'm Taylor."

"And I'm Campbell."

"I cast you, Taylor, as the understudy, because although you have a beautiful voice and so much potential, you don't project your voice well yet, and you don't seem to be very comfortable center stage."

"It's true," Taylor admitted. "I'm not."

"And you, Campbell—you might not have realized this yet, but you're a natural actress." Ms. Natasha smiled. "You're also a terrific friend."

She leaned back in her chair. "I'm going to speak to Priti about her role. I have a strong hunch this is all going to work out just fine. Priti's lucky to have friends who care about her so much."

Zoey felt a little better, although she wouldn't stop worrying about Priti until her friend was back to her normal, outgoing self.

"Zoey, I've got one thing to ask you before you go," said Ms. Natasha.

"What's that?" Zoey asked.

"The camp director told me about your blog, Sew Zoey, and I was hoping to get you to design some really fabulous new costumes for the main characters," Ms. Natasha said. "We've got costumes for the cast, but I'd love to get some fresh ideas for the leads, to change it up a bit. Because the costumes I have are a bit more modern in style, I'm thinking of changing the setting from ancient Greece to something a bit more contemporary. What do you think?"

"Sounds cool!" Zoey exclaimed. "I'd love to design the costumes. Plus, I haven't been sewing at all, which feels really weird."

"Great!" declared Ms. Natasha. "I'm so glad we had this little chat."

"Me too," Zoey said.

"Me three," Taylor said, nodding enthusiastically. She was staring at Zoey with wide eyes.

As soon as they left the director's office, Taylor grabbed Zoey's arm.

"Wait . . . are you *the* Zoey? From the Sew Zoey blog?" she asked.

"Um . . . yes. That's me," Zoey said.

"I can't believe it!" Taylor said. "I read your blog all the time! My friend Kaley told me about it, and now I read it every chance I get."

"In fact," Campbell added, "right before we came to camp, Taylor and I were thinking about writing to you for fashion advice!"

"Wow! Well, now you don't have to write to me—you can just ask me in person," Zoey said.

"We'll do that," Campbell said. "But first things first. We need to go cheer up Priti."

------------ CHAPTER 10 ------------

Dramarama

Dear Kate,

Hi hi hi hi!! I can't remember which sport you're doing this week, but I hope you're having a blast kicking, paddling, or whatever. You wrote me about running five miles a day. I can't imagine having to run five miles ever, especially when it's this hot! How do you survive? I'm glad to hear you get to go swimming, too. I was picturing you melting into a puddle of hot, tired, Kate goo at the end of the day.

Priti's down about not getting the lead in a play. Do you have any good coach things I can tell her to cheer her up? I'm trying to think of what Dad would say. I'm attaching a sketch of the outfit I came up with for her character. Hope it makes her like the whole play situation more! Miss you!!

Xoxo,

Zoey

Fortunately, it wasn't in Priti's nature to be down for long. Once the director spoke to her and explained why she cast Priti in the part of Puck, she cheered up quickly and was soon back to her usual self. She was still envious that Campbell was going to get to kiss Nick, but since Campbell clearly wasn't looking forward to it, it wasn't something Priti was going to let come between their friendship.

The camp days took on a fun routine. Mornings were for nature walks, arts and crafts, sports, and other activities, and afternoons were spent at rehearsals for the theater production. Priti, having reconciled herself to her role, was absolutely shining as Puck. Zoey sat in on rehearsals with her sketchbook to get ideas. Ms. Natasha brainstormed with Zoey about what contemporary setting might allow her to create the most interesting costumes. Zoey thought of her recent visit to New York and all the varied fashions she'd seen there.

"And then the woods could be Central Park!" she suggested.

"I love it!" Ms. Natasha said. "What a fabulous idea. And we can make great sets for that, too. Go for it."

Zoey took measurements for the main characters' costumes. Her favorite was Priti's. It was whimsical and woodsy, to tie into the Central

Park theme, but Zoey made sure to add a bunch of sparkly sequins to catch the light—and to make Priti happy, of course!

Time at camp passed by quickly. Zoey was busy creating costumes for the lead characters, and she spent a lot of time using the sewing machine in the arts and crafts room.

Weekends were a time for sports and relaxation. One Sunday, Zoey and Priti agreed to meet Campbell and Taylor at the lake after lunch for a cool-down swim, because it was so hot and humid.

"After we call our mom," Taylor said. "We call every Sunday. She'd worry if we didn't."

"Plus, it's nice to hear her voice, you know, even though it makes me a little homesick," Campbell said. "A swim will cheer me right up!"

Priti and Zoey walked down to the lake and found a good spot for their towels.

"Are you glad you came to camp, even though my dad kind of made you do it?" Priti asked as they stretched out to soak up the sun.

"He didn't *make* me do anything—but I *am* really glad he suggested it," Zoey said. "I'm having so much fun. How 'bout you?"

"I'm having fun too," Priti said. "And it'll be totally worth it if my parents are happier when I get back. It's been scary to see them argue so much. I've been really afraid they were going to get a divorce."

"I know," Zoey said. "But . . . I'm sure this break will be good for them."

The truth was, Zoey wasn't sure at all. Her dad had said they'd just have to wait and see. But she wanted everything to go well, for Priti's sake, because she knew how worried her friend was.

It wasn't long before Taylor and Campbell joined them. They were dressed in matching swimsuits, matching flip-flops, and matching swim caps. Priti and Zoey started laughing.

"It's Camplor and Taybell!" Priti said. "Honestly, when the two of you are together and dressed exactly the same like that, it's impossible to tell who is who!"

"Is there some kind of secret to telling you two apart?" Zoey asked. "Like, does one of you have a freckle or a scar the other one doesn't have?"

"Well . . . at the moment, Campbell has bangs, but I don't," Taylor said. "Mom still hasn't recovered from that."

"Wait—what bangs?" Zoey asked. "You don't have bangs."

"I do. You just can't see them," Campbell said. She pulled out shorter strands of hair from her French braid.

"See, I cut them myself," Campbell admitted. "I was just sick of everyone mistaking me for Taylor. But ever since the Day of the Hair Hacking, Mom's made us both wear our hair in French braids, so no one can tell."

"I can't remember ever not being dressed alike." Taylor sighed. "We've worn the same thing—from our hair down to our shoes—ever since we were little."

"It's not that we don't like being twins," Campbell said. "Being identical can be fun. We used to switch places sometimes, but even that's getting old. We're tired of looking like clones."

"That's what I was going to write to Sew Zoey—I

mean, to you—about," Taylor confessed. "I wanted to ask for advice about finding clothes that look similar enough to keep Mom happy but that are still different enough to let Campbell and me feel like ourselves."

"It does get confusing with the two of you dressed the same," Priti agreed.

"I would love to help you," Zoey said. "It'll be fun!"

"Really?" Taylor said. "That would be awesome. I can't wait!"

While the girls were basking in the sun after swimming in the lake, Zoey asked the twins questions. Did they prefer wearing pants, shorts, or skirts? Taylor loved wearing skirts, but Campbell felt more comfortable in pants and shorts. She also asked them about their favorite hobbies and sports and which colors they liked best.

Even though the twins were identical, their tastes weren't. Taylor's favorite color was blue, and Campbell's was green. Zoey had a lot to work with.

That night, Zoey curled on her bunk with the journal and pencils that had been a gift from her dad and aunt Lulu, and worked on ideas for the twins' clothes. She tried to create outfits that were different enough to let each girl express herself, but which still had some elements that brought them together to show that they were proud to be twins.

At breakfast the next morning, she revealed the designs she'd come up with. The twins were thrilled.

"Oh my gosh, Zoey! You're amazing!" Taylor exclaimed. "I love mine!"

"I love mine too!" Campbell said. "I wish I could wear it right now."

"If I were at home, I could make them for you, no problem," Zoey said. "But I don't have my sewing machine. Camp rules."

"Can you make them for us when you get home, if we send you the money for materials?" Taylor asked, gazing longingly at the sketches. "If Mom saw us in those outfits, maybe she'd realize we don't always have to be dressed like two peas in a pod."

"Sure," Zoey said, but she'd just had another idea—one she had to keep secret until she'd had a chance to speak to Ms. Natasha.

As soon as she had a spare moment, Zoey went to the theater building to see the director. She explained Campbell and Taylor's lookalike dilemma and how they wanted to convince their mother it was time for them to choose their own clothes. Then Zoey showed Ms. Natasha the designs she'd created for the twins.

"I just think if I could make the outfits for them to wear when their mom comes to pick them up, maybe it'll help her change her mind," Zoey explained. "But it would mean I'd have to use the camp's sewing machine and some of your fabrics. I brought some of my own fabrics from home, but not enough, and besides, they're not what I have in mind for this. I'd do it all in my spare time."

"I don't think that will be a problem, Zoey," Ms. Natasha said. "After all, designing and making clothes is a terrific arts and crafts project!"

"Thank you!" Zoey said. She couldn't wait to get started on the surprise project for her twin friends.

Zoey decided to let Priti in on the secret, so she could help Zoey pick fabrics and consult on the design—and because it was more fun collaborating on a surprise project than having to keep it all to herself. It felt so great to be sewing again that Zoey was able to make the outfits in no time at all.

"I wanted to keep this a secret till the last minute, but we have to let the twins in on this," Zoey told Priti one afternoon, after showing her the almost-finished pieces. "I need them for fittings now. I got a sense of their size by taking measurements from Campbell's clothes when she wasn't in the cabin, but to get these outfits perfect, I need to see them on."

"Oooh! Can I be there when you tell them?" Priti exclaimed. "I want to see the identical expressions on their identical faces!"

Zoey caught Taylor and Campbell before rehearsal, making sure Priti was on hand.

"Can you two stick around for a few minutes after rehearsal? I need to do a fitting," she said.

The twins looked puzzled.

"But I thought you already finished our costumes," Taylor said.

"It's not for that," Zoey said. "It's for a little surprise I've been working on."

"Surprise?" Campbell asked, and then smiled widely. "Wait! Do you mean . . . the outfits?"

Zoey nodded, grinning from ear to ear.

"Seriously?!" Taylor shrieked. "I'm so excited!!"

"Me too!" Campbell exclaimed. "But how?"

"Priti's been helping me," Zoey said. "And Ms. Natasha let me use the theater department's sewing machine and fabrics. We wanted you to be able to wear the outfits when your mom comes to pick you up from camp!"

"I can't believe you two went to so much trouble for us," Taylor said.

"You guys are the best," Campbell agreed. "I'm so glad you came to Blue Mountain this summer."

"Let's just hope your mom is glad too," Zoey said. "After rehearsal, you can try them on and I'll make them fit just right."

CHAPTER 11

Not Exactly Two Peas in a Pod

Dear Libby,

Bonjour! I'm glad to hear ballet camp is *très magnifique!* I'm sure your feet are sore after dancing all day. I'm not sure which is worse—sore toes or itchy mosquito bites. Neither is a whole lot of fun. . . .

Not long now till I see you! We have to go to the beach, and then to the pool, and back to the beach, and then to the mall. Especially the mall, since there won't be mosquitoes there. Ha-ha!

Remember the identical twins I told you about in my last letter? They usually wear identical outfits, too, but I made these new clothes for them. They'll still be dressed twinish but also look a little unique. Or that's what I'm hoping!

Can't wait to see you and catch up on everything!

Xoxo,

Zoey

"Can you believe there's only a week left?" asked Kelly, descending from her bunk bed. "It seems like we just got here."

Zoey knew exactly how she felt. When her dad

had talked about going to camp for six weeks, it had seemed like such a long time to be away from home and her friends. But it had flown by, and now it almost seemed like it was going to end too soon.

There were so many more things she wanted to try. She still hadn't done archery yet, or canoeing. But she'd had a great time exploring all the arts and crafts offered—tie-dyeing, ceramics, jewelry design, stained glass—and of course, making the costumes for the play.

"Yikes!" Campbell's face suddenly looked pale. "That means only one week till the play."

"I can't wait to see you in it," Marisol said. "Zoey says you're amazing."

"Oh, um . . . thanks," Campbell said softly.

Campbell sounds strange, Zoey thought. She'd have to ask her if everything was okay at breakfast.

They met Priti and Taylor in the dining hall, as usual. As soon as they'd all sat down, Campbell said, "So, I'm really nervous."

"About what?" Priti asked.

"About kissing Nick in the play," Campbell confessed. "It's so *awkward*. I mean, I know it's just a quick peck, but . . . what happens if I start giggling? Or even worse, if I *miss his face entirely*!"

"I could kiss him for you," Priti offered. "Nick's *sooooo* dreamy."

"I wish you could." Campbell cracked a smile. "I'm totally dreading it."

"Well . . . my aunt Lulu always says 'fake it till you make it,'" Zoey said.

"What does that mean?" Taylor asked.

"Basically, if you pretend you feel totally comfortable kissing Nick, maybe, eventually, you'll actually feel that way," Zoey explained.

"The play's only a week away," Campbell said. "It would take years of faking it before I'd be able to convince myself that kissing anyone in front of all those people is no big deal."

"I don't know if this helps, but one of the reasons I love acting is that it gives me the chance to be someone different for just for a little while— kind of like trying on a new hat," Priti said. "So maybe pretend to be someone glamorous who thinks that kissing Nick is just, you know, *ho-hum*. And try to have fun with it. But not *too much* fun, because I have a crush on him!"

Campbell actually relaxed enough to laugh.

"Really? I had no idea," Campbell joked. "Seriously, though, thanks, guys. Okay, I feel a little better now. Still nervous, but at least I have a plan."

Before they knew it, it was the night of the performance—which was also the last night of camp. The parents of the cast and crew had driven up early. They were staying nearby and would come pick up their campers the next day. When Priti's parents arrived, Zoey noticed they weren't arguing. In fact, they were smiling at each other and even laughing instead of being tense and angry-looking like they'd been the last few months when she'd seen them. She hoped that was a good sign. Zoey's dad was there, too, even though she wasn't performing. He wanted to see her costumes and cheer on Priti.

When the curtain went up, the sets looked wonderful—all the stage crew's hard work to re-create the New York skyline and Central Park had paid off. Priti shone in her role as Puck, and

Zoey's costumes looked amazing. Campbell was fantastic as Titania. *Ms. Natasha is right,* Zoey thought. *She really is a natural actress.*

Then it was time for *the kiss.* Zoey had her fingers crossed and held her breath, hoping Campbell wouldn't start giggling. Luckily, she didn't—but Nick did. He burst into a fit of uncontrollable laughter as he leaned in to kiss Campbell.

Campbell was a total professional. She didn't break character at all when Nick laughed. She waited for him to pull himself together, and when he finally gave her a quick peck, she carried on with the next line.

When the play ended, the applause was deafening. Priti and Campbell both got standing ovations. Ms. Natasha called Zoey out onto the stage, so she could be acknowledged for making the beautiful new costumes for the lead actors.

The cheers took Zoey by surprise. She was used to getting compliments on her blog, but those were typed messages. It was hard to imagine that those messages were from real people. But this was real clapping from lots of real people in the audience!

Even though she still preferred life behind the curtains, she started to understand why Priti enjoyed life in the spotlight so much. It was fun to get applause and to get immediate feedback, especially when it was so positive! Maybe this was what Daphne Shaw felt like when she came on the runway to join the models at the end of her runway show at Fashion Week!

After the performance, the Holbrookes and Mr. Webber came together to greet Zoey and Priti.

"You were incredible, Priti," Mr. Holbrooke said, giving her a big bouquet of flowers. "A real leading lady."

"Our star," Mrs. Holbrooke said, give her daughter a hug. "I couldn't be more proud, sweetie!"

Priti beamed, looking from her mom to her dad.

"Thanks!" she said. "So . . . did you sort everything out while I was gone?"

Zoey was surprised her friend just came out and asked her parents the question right away, but she knew it was the only thing on her friend's mind. After all, it was the reason Priti and Zoey had both come to camp in the first place, even though they'd ended up having a wonderful time.

There was a split second of hesitation before Priti's mom said, "Yes, honey. We did sort things out."

"We can catch up later. Don't you two have a cast party to get to?" Mr. Holbrooke asked.

"Yes, we do," Zoey said. "And you guys have the parents' dinner." She gave her dad a big hug. "I've missed you," she said. "And Marcus."

"We've missed you, too," her dad said. "It's been very quiet around the house with you gone."

"Don't worry," Zoey said. "I'll be back tomorrow to make things noisy again. So, is Aunt Lulu still dating New Boyfriend John?"

"Yes, she is!" Dad said. "She cooked him dinner the other night."

"Cooking? Sounds serious!" Zoey said with a smile.

"See you tomorrow after breakfast," Priti called out cheerfully to her parents as she and Zoey ran off to the cast party.

"Oh my gosh. Did you see how much happier my parents looked?" Priti asked as they walked into the cast party.

"Yeah, they were both smiling and laughing a lot," Zoey said. "I haven't seen them doing that in a while."

"See! It worked! We had a great time at camp this summer *and* now my parents are falling back in love with each other!" Priti said. "Thanks for coming with me, Zo. You're the best bestie ever!"

"I'm glad I came," Zoey said. "And if it helped your parents, then that's the icing on the cake."

"The icing on the wedding cake?" Priti asked, whistling "The Wedding March."

Zoey glanced over at Taylor and Campbell, whose mom was giving them a group hug.

"I just hope the twins' mom likes their new outfits tomorrow," Zoey said.

"She *has* to love them," Priti said. "How could she not? They rock!"

"We'll see . . . ," Zoey said.

But she didn't spend too much time worrying, because it was time for the cast party—pizza and soda to celebrate the successful performance. Everyone was in high spirits, especially when Ms. Natasha led them in a medley of show tunes.

After the cast party, they joined the rest of the camp down by the lake for one last bonfire and a few too many last s'mores.

When the fire began to burn low and it was time to return to their cabins, Priti and Zoey grabbed their flashlights and started walking back together. Zoey had to stop and tie her shoelace, and Priti, who was ahead of her on the path, didn't realize it and kept walking. When Zoey looked up, she saw someone approach Priti but couldn't tell who it was in the darkness.

"Ooh, Nick, you scared me!" Priti said.

"Oh my gosh, sorry," Nick said. "I . . . uh . . . just wanted to tell you . . . how great you were . . . in the show."

Zoey couldn't see it in the dim light, but knowing her friend, she was sure Priti's face had turned pink.

"Th-thanks. You were great too."

"Can I . . . walk you back to your cabin?" Nick asked.

Priti looked back over her shoulder toward where Zoey was hidden in the shadows.

"Okay," she said.

Zoey breathed a sigh of relief. And then she saw Nick take Priti's hand. She felt awkward about being an inadvertent fly on the wall, but she was really excited for Priti!

After waiting for a minute or two to give the pair time to walk far enough ahead, she walked back to her cabin by herself. Campbell was already there, getting into her pj's.

"Guess who's walking Priti back to her cabin!" Zoey said. "*Nick!!*"

Campbell's eyes lit up and she grinned. "That's awesome! I hope we don't have to wait till breakfast to find out what happens."

"Me neither," Zoey said. "The suspense is killing me!"

Luckily, it wasn't long before there was a knock on the cabin door, and Priti stood there, flushed and beaming.

Priti, Campbell, and Zoey all squealed at the same time.

"What happened?!" Zoey asked.

"He is *sooooo* sweet." Priti sighed. "He gave me a little kiss on the cheek—and he didn't laugh this time."

"See, it was you he wanted to kiss all along," Campbell said.

Priti twirled around in a circle.

"I think you're right." She sighed again. "But why did he have to wait until the last night of camp to do it?"

"Maybe he was shy," Campbell said. "Maybe he wasn't sure if you liked him."

"But I do like him!" Priti said.

"Well, duh!" Zoey said.

"And then he asked me if I was planning to come back to camp next year. Well . . . *now* I am, definitely!"

It seemed like all was well that ended well as far Priti was concerned, Zoey thought. Now she just had to see how things went the next morning with the twins and their mom.

Zoey was so excited to get dressed the next morning. She was going to be sad to say good-bye to the new friends she'd made at camp, but she was definitely *not* going to be the teensiest bit sorry to say good-bye to her uniform! The thought of a whole closetful of colorful clothes and being able to pick a new outfit every day was heavenly. She was slipping on her shoes when Campbell tapped her on the shoulder.

"How do I look?" Campbell asked Zoey and everyone in the cabin. She was wearing the outfit Zoey designed, walking up and down the narrow space between the bunks as if she were on a catwalk. Her smile was brighter than ever.

"Like a model," Marisol said. "Your mom will love it!"

"I hope so," Zoey whispered.

"Hey, Zoey, can you redesign the camp uniforms, too?" Kelly asked, throwing hers into her trunk in disgust. "I get so sick of wearing that ugly thing."

"Maybe next year," Zoey said, smiling.

After breakfast, when it was time to go meet the parents in the parking lot, Campbell and Taylor asked Zoey to come with them to meet their mother.

"Maybe she'll want to meet you," Taylor said. "Seeing as you designed the outfits, and all. Then again, maybe she won't."

"Okay," Zoey said.

She couldn't believe how nervous the two girls were to wear nonmatching clothes. Her dad let her wear what she wanted. She couldn't imagine always having to dress like Marcus!

The twins' mother stood by her SUV. When she turned and caught a glimpse of Campbell and Taylor in their new outfits, the shock registered on her face. She didn't look upset, but she didn't look happy.

"Girls!" she exclaimed, hugging both of them. "What . . . are you . . . wearing?"

"New outfits. Our friend Zoey designed them for us," Taylor said. She sounded nervous. "Zoey's kind of famous. She has her own fashion blog."

"Don't you like them, Mom?" Campbell added.

"*We* love them," Taylor said, sounding less nervous and more determined.

"I . . . I love them too," their mother said. "I guess I'm just a little *surprised*, that's all."

"Mom, we're tired of being dressed the same all the time," Campbell said.

"We like being twins, but we need a chance to be ourselves," Taylor pleaded. "I don't want to always wear the same thing as Campbell. Say it's okay, *please*?"

"Of course it's okay, sweetie," their mom said. "You know, I never realized you girls were so upset about being dressed alike. I just automatically buy two of everything, just like I have since you were born. It's habit more than anything."

She put her arms around her identical daughters.

"I'm glad you want to express your individual personalities," she said. "You've always been totally different, unique girls to me."

"So why did you freak out so much when Campbell cut her hair?" Taylor asked.

"Well, most of all, because she did it herself without asking me for permission," her mom said. "And also because I'm not a big fan of bangs or anything that would cover up your beautiful eyes."

"So if I'd asked you first, you wouldn't have been mad?" Campbell said.

"No. I might have tried to talk you out of bangs, but maybe we could have come up with a compromise," her mom said.

"I'm sorry, Mom," Campbell said, hugging her mother. "Next time I'll talk to you first."

"And I'm sorry for making you two dress alike all these years. I guess I thought you liked it," their mom said. "Zoey, thanks for opening my eyes and for making such great outfits for my girls."

"It was fun," Zoey said. "And I'm soooo glad you like the clothes."

"You know what, Mom? Earlier this summer, Zoey got to meet Daphne Shaw!" Taylor said.

"Really?" her mom said. "I've got a few Daphne Shaw pieces. I love her designs."

It was the perfect ending to a great camp experience. Zoey waved good-bye to her friends, and went to find her father. It had been a really fun summer, but she was ready to go home.

CHAPTER 12

Let There Be Internet!

I'm back! I never thought I'd survive six whole weeks without my phone and my computer and the Internet, but it actually wasn't so bad. I did miss you all, but now I just have more to tell you about all our amazing adventures. Camp was awesome! I had so much fun and enjoyed making new friends, but I think I'm more of a city girl than a nature girl at heart. Still, going to new places and trying different things gives me lots of ideas for designs. Here's my latest!

"Yum!" Zoey said after her first forkful of pancake. "I've *really* missed your cooking, Dad!"

"You missed Dad's pancakes more than you missed your fantastic, amazing, wonderful brother?" Marcus asked, pouting.

"Or your wonderful aunt and her incredibly adorable dog?" Aunt Lulu asked.

Buttons sat next to Zoey, looking up with her big brown eyes and wagging her tail across the floor. She *was* incredibly adorable.

"I missed all of you!" Zoey said. "Especially Buttons. But at least the people at camp were nice—which is more than I can say for the food."

"It definitely wasn't the same around here without you, Zo," Aunt Lulu said. "We all missed you."

"We sure did," Dad agreed. "I had no one to tell me what to wear."

"And you should have seen some of the outfits he came up with," Aunt Lulu said, giggling. "Your fashion emergency alarm would have been sounding full blast!"

"I had to invite Allie over to give him pointers," Marcus said.

"I'm sure that wasn't the *only* reason you invited Allie over," Zoey said, smiling.

"Well, okay, we might have also watched a movie," Marcus admitted.

"Can someone drive me to The Perfect Ten later?" Zoey asked. "Libby, Kate, Priti, and I are going to have a reunion over pedicures. It feels like *forever* since I've seen Kate and Libby!"

"I'll drop you off on the way home," Aunt Lulu said.

"But first I need another pancake. Or two," Zoey said. "I've got a lot of good eating to catch up on."

Kate and Libby were already choosing toenail colors at The Perfect Ten when Aunt Lulu dropped off Zoey.

"Zoey!" they exclaimed when they saw her, and the three girls embraced.

"So tell me everything, guys! How was your summer?" Zoey asked.

"Ballet camp was fun, but it was really hard work," Libby said. "We danced for, like, four hours a day! My feet got really beat-up. I seriously need a pedicure!"

"Me too," Zoey said. "After six weeks in the woods, my toes are looking grody."

"Me three," Kate said. "Playing sports all summer doesn't exactly make for pretty feet."

"Where's Priti?" Zoey asked. "She's late."

The owner of The Perfect Ten asked if they were ready for their pedicures.

"What should we do?" Libby asked. "Go ahead?"

"I guess we should at least get started," Zoey said. "I'll text Priti and see if she can hurry."

When the girls were seated in the pedicure chairs, Kate said, "Enough about us, Zoey. Tell me all about your visit with Daphne Shaw!"

Zoey was more than happy to share with her best friend the details of one of the best days of her life.

"The T-shirt I'm wearing was a present from

Daphne," she said. "And she gave me this note with it."

She scrolled to the picture she'd taken of Daphne's note, so that she could reread it whenever she needed encouragement, and handed her phone to Kate.

Kate read the note aloud.

> Dear Zoey,
> I hope you had a great time today and that you'll keep in touch. We fashion sisters have to stick together!
> Fondly,
> Daphne

"Huh . . . that's odd." Kate chuckled.

"What's odd?" Zoey asked.

"How Daphne Shaw calls you 'fashion sisters,'" Kate said. "It reminds me of your fashion fairy god-mother, Fashionsista."

It was as if, all of a sudden, puzzle pieces suddenly clicked into place in Zoey's head. She'd thought the handwriting on Daphne's note looked vaguely familiar.

"Wait—hand me my phone," she told Kate.

Zoey scrolled to the picture of herself and Daphne that her father had taken in Daphne's office. She zoomed in on Daphne's wrist and saw . . .

"I don't believe it! She's wearing a sticks-and-stones bracelet, exactly like the one Fashionsista sent me when I was getting nasty comments on Sew Zoey!" Zoey exclaimed.

"No way," Kate said, clasping her hand over her mouth.

"Must be a coincidence," Libby added. "It *is* the coolest bracelet!"

"And I saw her slipping something shiny into her desk drawer when she thought I wasn't looking. . . . Could it have been the bracelet?" Zoey wondered. "I don't remember her wearing a bracelet at lunch later that day."

"Are you sure?" Libby asked.

"Pretty sure," Zoey said. And then she remembered something else about lunch. "Oh! And after lunch she was reapplying her lip gloss, and she had the exact same brand of 'lucky lip gloss' that Fashionsista sent me before I appeared on *Fashion Showdown*. How much of a coincidence is *that*?!"

"I think it's too much of a coincidence to be a coincidence," Kate said.

"Could Daphne and Fashionsista be the same person?" Zoey asked. "How cool would it be if my fashion idol and my fashion fairy godmother were *both* Daphne Shaw? It would be the perfect ending for my perfect summer."

"A fashion fairy tale ending!" Kate giggled. "But Daphne is even better than a prince."

Zoey giggled too. "Well, a prince would be pretty nice too."

"I . . . well, I don't want to burst your bubble," Libby chimed in. "But couldn't Daphne and Zoey just have the same bracelet and lip gloss? Daphne could have read about it on your blog or a magazine. I bet she has dozens of lip glosses and bracelets, like my aunt. People who work in fashion get a lot of freebies."

"But why would she take off the bracelet when I got to the office?" Zoey asked.

"I don't know," Libby said. "Maybe she was allergic to it. My mom gets itchy from some kinds of jewelry."

"I guess that's possible," Zoey said.

"And why would she go to so much trouble to keep it all a secret?" Libby continued. "I just don't get it."

Zoey shrugged. "I have no idea, but—" She was interrupted by the jingle of the bell on the salon door.

"Oh, look, Priti's here!" Kate said.

"Hi, Priti!" Libby said. "Welcome back!"

But Priti looked awful; her face was pale and her eyes were puffy and bloodshot, as if she'd been doing a lot of crying.

"Is everything okay?" Zoey asked.

"No," Priti said, her eyes filling with tears. "Everything isn't okay. It might never be okay again. The whole summer at camp was a waste. My parents are getting a . . . a divorce!"

"Oh no!" Kate said.

"Priti, I'm so sorry," Libby said. "I . . . don't what to say."

"There's nothing *to* say," Priti said. "I feel so silly. I honestly thought they had fallen in love again. But we had a family meeting today, and they said they'd decided to split up. They arranged everything already, so there's no going back. Dad's moving out tomorrow. My life is over."

Zoey felt awful that the Holbrookes were getting divorced. Priti's life was going to change in ways none of them could imagine quite yet. But Zoey knew that as bad as things seemed, Priti's life wasn't totally over. They had to try to help Priti find her "glass half full" side. Since Priti's glass was usually either filled to the brim or overflowing, it was hard for her friends to see her feeling so down.

"I know it feels like it's over, Priti," Zoey said. "And I guess the part where the Holbrooke family all lives together in the same house will be over. But *your* life isn't over. It's just going to be . . . different."

"That's true," Kate said. "Lots of kids at school have parents who are divorced, and they're okay. They just . . . you know, have visitation schedules and spend one vacation with their dad and the other with their mom and get extra presents on their birthday."

"Maybe it's like when you move to a totally new place, like I did," Libby said. "You have to find your new normal."

"But I don't want a new normal," Priti wailed. "I like my old normal."

Zoey, Libby, and Kate exchanged worried glances.

"I guess things will change, but not completely. Your parents might not be together, but they love *you* as much as always. That won't ever change," Zoey reminded her friend.

"And we'll be here for you, too, always. That won't change either," Libby said, handing Priti some tissues to dry her eyes.

"Hey, I have an idea!" Kate said, going to pick out a different nail polish: a sparkly silver color. "Let's all get our toes painted in this color. Maybe when you see it, it'll remind you to hang on to your Priti sparkliness until things get better."

Priti wiped her eyes, blew her nose, and nodded.

"You know, you are *Priti* sparkly," Zoey said. "Get it? Pretty sparkly?"

Kate and Libby laughed, and Priti gave them a watery smile. "Yeah," Priti said. "But even if I can't feel sparkly all the time, I know I have the best besties around to help me get through this."

The girls all stood up and hugged Priti tightly in a group hug, and Priti took a few deep breaths and began to calm down. She plopped down in a pedicure chair next to her friends, and they all had their toes painted with silver sparkles—a nail polish that looked like Priti's usual personality in a bottle.

Zoey thought back to some of her sewing challenges over the past few months. None of them seemed as big or as difficult as what Priti was going through.

If only making Priti feel better was as easy sewing up a ripped seam, Zoey thought.

Unfortunately, life wasn't like that. There weren't always the fairy tale endings that Priti, Zoey, Kate, and Libby hoped for. But at least the four best friends had one another. And that was *knot* too shabby.

All's well that mends well!
Turn the page for a sneak
peek at the next book in the
Sew Zoey series:

SWATCH
OUT!

It's a Mystery!

You have NO idea how excited I am to be blogging again! After six weeks away at camp, being able to just pick up my laptop and blog whenever I want to feels AMAZING!

School's starting pretty soon, but there's enough summer left for a few small adventures, right? And even though my top priority is to be a good friend to one of my besties who really needs me at the moment, I've also got a mystery to solve. A *fashion* mystery. That's right! I *think* I've figured out the identity of my longtime "mysterious benefactor," Fashionsista. I'm still not sure how I feel about finding out for SURE who she is. After all, there's something pretty awesome about having a secret friend who sends you amazing gifts! But I think it's time. So, Fashionsista, if you're reading this, check your mailbox for a letter from me. I'll be mailing it to you just as soon as I get the courage to put it in the mailbox. . . . At least, I think it'll be to you!

And in honor of the potential unmasking of my secret friend, I've posted a sketch of a masquerade outfit. . . . isn't it dramatic? Probably too much for the first day of school, though, right?

Zoey Webber was having a blast. It had been way too long since she'd spent a lazy afternoon at the community pool with friends, and she'd even been lucky enough to get a ride there from her older brother, Marcus, who was working as a lifeguard for the summer.

Zoey and her friends Priti Holbrooke and Libby Flynn had found three lounge chairs near the diving well, and they were stretched out chatting. Libby was filling Priti and Zoey in on the details of her ballet camp after Priti and Zoey shared stories from their six weeks at sleepaway camp. The only thing that could have made the afternoon better was if their other friend, Kate Mackey, could have been there too. But she was at preseason swim camp for another week.

"Guys, I have to tell you something," Zoey whispered. The girls leaned in closer, sensing a secret coming. "My brother is *seriously* losing it."

Priti and Libby both swiveled their eyes toward Marcus, who was perched on the lifeguard stand by the lap lanes. He wore sunglasses and a visor, and he appeared to be watching some young kids in the shallow end.

Priti squinted. "He looks fine to me, Zoey. What do you mean?"

Zoey blew out a breath that made her bangs fly up in the air. "I mean, he's in total *la-la land* over my friend Allie. They've been dating all summer, and he's completely spacey all the time! I asked him to put my pool bag in the car this morning, when we were leaving, and instead of putting it in the car, he put it back up in my *room*. I was in the kitchen, so I didn't notice, and then halfway to the pool I realized it wasn't in the backseat! So now I don't have clothes to wear to meet Kate for ice cream later."

"Ah-HA! So *that's* why you texted me to bring an extra towel." Priti laughed loudly. "I figured you'd been sketching and just forgot to pack your stuff."

Zoey laughed too. "Well, I'm not saying that would never happen, but it didn't today. Allie called him right as we were leaving, and he got all distracted. And he's making my dad nuts because he's always texting with Allie during dinner."

"My parents *hate* that," Libby said. "I have to

leave my phone up in my room during dinner. They like meals to be for family conversation only."

At the word "family," Zoey noticed a shadow cross Priti's face. Priti's parents had just recently decided to divorce, and Zoey knew how hard Priti was taking it.

"You okay, Priti?" Zoey asked. Priti was normally the life of any party, louder and more cheerful and zanier than anyone else. But since she'd gotten the news from her parents, she'd been subdued.

Priti nodded, but her shoulders wiggled up and down too, so it was more of a shrug than a nod, and seemed to mean, *Sorta, but not really.*

"It's just so weird," Priti said. "I came home from camp, and my dad moved out, and now it's just me and Mom and my sisters at home. It was so fast! Like, blink—no more Dad."

Priti was sitting in the middle of the three girls, and without a word, Libby and Zoey leaned toward her and squashed her with a hug. It was a Priti sandwich, and after a few seconds, Priti had to burst out laughing.

Zoey pulled back and smiled. "We knew that

was in there somewhere! Should we sandwich you again?"

Priti held up a hand. "No, please! Just change the subject. I'm fine as long as you guys keep talking." She turned to Libby and patted her leg. "What's new with you, Libs? Tell me everything. Pirouettes, pliés?"

Libby—who was normally the sweet, easygoing one—surprised the girls by saying, "Well, actually, my little sister is driving me bonkers."

"You mean Sophie?" Zoey cocked her head, curiously. Sophie was little, only about six years old, and the girls hardly ever saw her. With the age difference, and Sophie still being in elementary school, their schedules just didn't intersect.

Libby nodded guiltily. "I feel terrible even saying it. But Sophie's really sensitive—like me, but even more so—and she cries all the time. I try to be understanding and help her, but she gets upset about literally *everything*. And we've been home together so much this summer!"

Priti grabbed Libby's hand sympathetically. "Just because you're sisters doesn't mean you have to like each other all the time! My older sisters drive me bonkers, too, and they're way past the crying phase. I think that's just how siblings are."

Zoey wanted to chime in too, but Marcus didn't really drive Zoey bonkers. He was a pretty great brother, actually. Although he *had* been pretty dopey for putting her pool bag back up in her room. But since he'd also given her a ride, and had been nice enough to agree to take her to meet Kate later, she decided it was a draw. He was still a good brother.

Libby sighed. "I know this sounds crazy, but I'm pretty excited for school to start in a few weeks, so I won't be home as much. Even homework seems better than calming Sophie down from yet another tantrum!"

The girls laughed, and Priti nodded. "I'm ready for school too. I need to get out of my house and stop thinking about my family problems!"

"Do you know what *I'm* looking forward to?" Zoey added. "Tomorrow night's Cody Calloway concert . . ."

CHLOE TAYLOR

learned to sew when she was a little girl. She loved watching her grandmother Louise turn a scrap of blue fabric into a simple-but-fabulous dress, nightgown, or even a bathing suit in an instant. It was magical! Now that she's grown up, she still loves fashion: it's like art that you can wear. This is her first middle grade series. She lives, writes, and window-shops in New York City.

NANCY ZHANG

is an illustrator and an art and fashion lover with a passion for all beautiful things. She has published her work in the art books *L'Oiseau Rouge* and *Street Impressions* and in various fashion magazines and on websites. Visit her at her blog: www.xiaoxizhang.com. She currently lives in Berlin, Germany.

Great stories are like great accessories: You can never have too many! Collect all the books in the Sew Zoey series:

Ready to Wear

On Pins and Needles

Lights, Camera, Fashion!

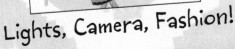

Stitches and
Stones

Cute as a Button

A Tangled Thread

Knot Too Shabby!